Henry Clinton

Observations on Some Parts of the Answer of Earl Cornwallis

to Sir Henry Clinton's Narrative

Henry Clinton

Observations on Some Parts of the Answer of Earl Cornwallis
to Sir Henry Clinton's Narrative

ISBN/EAN: 9783337091842

Printed in Europe, USA, Canada, Australia, Japan

Cover: Foto ©Andreas Hilbeck / pixelio.de

More available books at **www.hansebooks.com**

OBSERVATIONS

O N

Some Parts of Earl Cornwallis's Anfwer

T O

Sir Henry Clinton's Narrative.

B Y

LIEUTENANT-GENERAL
SIR HENRY CLINTON, K. B.

WHEN I publifhed a Narrative of my
conduct during the period of my command in
North America, which comprehends the
campaign of 1781, I was in hopes I had faid
every thing that was requifite to explain the
motives of my own actions, and to convince

b   every

every unprejudiced perſon, that certain poſi-
tions reſpecting them, advanced in Lord
Cornwallis's letter to me of the 20th of October, had no foundation. But it gives me
extreme concern to obſerve, that his Lordſhip's ſeeming to avow nearly the ſame ſentiments in his Introduction to a late publica-
tion, ſtyled, an Anſwer to that Narrative,
lays me under the neceſſity of troubling the
public again upon a ſubject, which they are
probably tired of; and I ſincerely wiſhed to
have done with. I hope, therefore, it may
not be judged improper to requeſt their attention to the following Obſervations on ſome
of the opinions and aſſertions therein ſtated.
Which (to be as conciſe as poſſible) I ſhall
take according to the order in which they
occur; — adding only, in an Appendix, the
copies of ſuch extracts from my correſpondence, and other papers, as appear neceſſary.

I find upon enquiry that the four letters
were omitted to be ſent to the Secretary of
State, which Lord Cornwallis mentions to
have been wanting when the papers relating
to this buſineſs were laid before the Houſe of
Lords. But the reaſons for his Lordſhip's
                                        march

march from Crofs-creek to Wilmington, and from thence into Virginia (ftated in the firft of them) had been before given in his letters of the 23d and 24th of April, to the Secretary of State, General Phillips, and myfelf; and thefe ftand the firft of thofe letters from his Lordfhip's correfpondence, read before the Houfe of Lords; the other three letters had been inferted in a pamphlet containing ex-tracts from our correfpondence, handed about at the time of the enquiry; and one of thofe pamphlets had been prefented, by my order, to Lord Townfhend, as a man of honour, and a friend to both parties, previous (I believe) to his noticing this omiffion to the Houfe; and all the four miffing letters were foon after publifhed in the Parliamentary Regifter, along with thofe which had been read to the Lords. So that Lord Cornwallis could not well have fuftained any injury by that omiffion. This, however, cannot be faid to have been the cafe with mine of the 30th of November, and 2d of December to his Lordfhip, and of the 6th of December to the American Minifter; which were with-held, whilft Lord Corn-wallis's letters of the 20th of October, and 2d

of

of December (to which they were anfwers)
were fuffered to operate, for a long time, upon
the minds of the public, to my prejudice.

My letters of the 30th of November and 2d
of December, were in Lord Cornwallis's poffeffion, when his friend, Lord Townfhend,
moved for thofe of his Lordfhip, which he
judged neceffary to explain his conduct. The
public will judge, whether mine were not, at
leaft, equally fo, to explain mine; and whether, on finding that the Secretary of State
had omitted to produce them to the Lords,
Lord Cornwallis ought not to have defired
Lord Townfhend to have moved for them.
I declare, I would have done fo, had I been
in his Lordfhip's place.

The four other letters, taken notice of by
Lord Cornwallis, were certainly not delivered
to him before November; becaufe the three
firft, having been committed to the charge of
General Leflie, (who was in a manner embarked for the Chefapeak, from the beginning
of Auguft to the arrival of the French fleet)
could not have been tranfmitted to his Lordfhip
fooner; and the laft (the fubftance of which,
however, had been previoufly communicated

in

in the prefence of a council of war, for his
Lordfhip's information to Major Cockran, who
joined him on the 9th of October) being fent
by an advice boat, did not reach the Chefapeak
before his furrender.   But whoever will take
the trouble of perufing thofe letters, will
perceive that his Lordfhip's conduct (in the
then ftate of matters) could not have been influenced by an earlier receipt of them.

Every man of fenfibility muft lament that
Lord Cornwallis has fo indifcreetly availed
himfelf of the liberty, he fuppofed was given
him, by the late change in American meafures.
For as *my fecret and moft private letter* to General
Phillips, dated April 30, contained nothing
neceffary for his Lordfhip's juftification ;   the
publifhing it was highly impolitic at leaft, not
to fay more — for reafons too obvious to need
explanation.

No perfon can be more ready than I am to
admit the difficulties Lord Cornwallis had to
ftruggle with ; and I fhall always acknowledge
that I expected fuccefs (notwithftanding) from
his Lordfhip's abilities.   I left his Lordfhip
in the Carolinas, with every power, civil and
military, which I could give him, to carry on
fuch

such operations as he should judge moſt
likely to complete their reduction. Where I
had hopes of ſucceſs, I ſtudiouſly ſought to
approve without reſerve. And, as long as I
imagined his Lordſhip to be in ſufficient force,
and in other reſpects prepared and competent to
give the experiment of ſupporting our friends
in North Carolina, *a fair and ſolid trial*, I certainly approved. But after the unfortunate
day of *Cowpens*, which diminiſhed his Lordſhip's acting army nearly one fourth ; and after
he thought proper to deſtroy great part of his
waggons, proviant train, &c. (whereby he
was reduced, I fear, to ſomething too like a
Tartar move) ; had it then been poſſible for
him to have conſulted me, he would have
found that, could I have even *conſented* to his
perſiſting in his march into that province, that
conſent muſt have totally reſted upon the
high opinion I entertained of his Lordſhip's
exertions, and not on any other flattering proſpect I had of ſucceſs.

Major Fergufon's misfortune was one of
thoſe untoward circumſtances, which Lord
Cornwallis ſays, occured during the four
months ſucceeding the battle of Camden. His
Lordſhip,

Lordſhip, immediately after the complete victory he there obtained, ordered our friends in
North Carolina, to arm and intercept the
beaten army of General Gates; promiſing
them at the ſame time, that he would march
directly to the borders of that province in their
ſupport.   About this time Major Ferguſon
was detached to a diſtance from his Lordſhip,
with a body of militia (without being ſupported
by regular troops) under an idea that he could
make them fight ; notwithſtanding his Lordſhip had informed me, ſome little time before,
that it was contrary to the experience of the
army, as well as of Major Ferguſon himſelf.
The conſequence was, that the Major and his
whole corps were unfortunately maſſacred.
Lord Cornwallis was, immediately upon hearing of this event, obliged to quit the borders of
North Carolina, and leave our friends there at
the mercy of an inveterate enemy, whoſe power
became irreſiſtible by this neceſſary retreat.
This fatal cataſtrophe, moreover, loſt his Lordſhip the whole militia of Ninety-ſix, amounting
to four thouſand men, and even threw South
Carolina into a ſtate of confuſion and rebellion.

wallis

How nearly the force I left with Lord Cornwallis in the Southern diftrict, and what I afterwards fent to him, might have been adequate or not to the fuccefs expected from it, I fhall not now examine. It was all I could poffibly fpare. But for the fatisfaction of the public, I fhall give at the end of the Appendix, a view of the force firft left with his Lordfhip, of what was fent to him afterwards, and of what was finally under his Lordfhip's orders throughout the whole extent of his command; — to contraft with which, I fhall add alfo another view of the force left under my own immediate orders at New York, at different periods; giving at the fame time as near a calculation as I can make from the intelligence received, of the number of regular troops which the enemy had oppofed to each of us. I beg leave likewife to mention, that before I failed from Charles-town, I offered to Lord Cornwallis all he wifhed, all he wanted, of every fort; and that his Lordfhip expreffed himfelf to be perfectly fatisfied with the troops he had, and wifhed for no more, as will appear from the letters annexed. What the exact ftrength of the corps under his Lordfhip's immediate command may have been at any given

period,

period, I. cannot ascertain, as I had not regular returns of them; but his Lordship did not make any complaint to me of the smallness of his force when he commenced his move into North Carolina; and I always thought it to be full as large as I had rated it at.

I cannot judge of the assurances of co-operation which Lord Cornwallis may have received from our friends in North Carolina, but from his Lordship's report; and his Lordship best knows, whether *he received any after the effects of Major Ferguson's misfortune were known.* But his Lordship cannot forget that our friends, who had risen by his order, were left exposed to ruin by his retreat, and numbers of them actually massacred. I am therefore at a loss to guess what may have been his Lordship's reasons for being surprized that they failed to join him after the victory at Guildford; as such effort of loyalty could scarcely be expected from them after their past sufferings, when they saw his Lordship's army so greatly reduced. after the action, and so scantily supplied with provisions; which, without doubt was very far short of that solid support which they had been encouraged to expect from his

Lordship's

Lordſhip's promiſes. And indeed his Lordſhip might have ſuppoſed that theſe were their
ſentiments from what followed, as deſcribed
by himſelf. "Many of the inhabitants rode
" into camp, ſhook me by the hand, ſaid
" they were glad to ſee us, and to hear we had
" beat Greene, and then rode home again ;"—
no doubt with aching hearts, from the melan-
choly ſecene his Lordſhip's camp "_encumbered_
"_with a long train of ſick and wounded_," ex-
hibited to their view.

But as this attempt (ſuch as it was) had
failed, ſurely Lord Cornwallis's next object
ſhould have been, _to ſecure South Carolina:_ and
this appears to have been his Lordſhip's own
opinion when he wrote his letter to General
Leſlie of the 12th of December, 1780: —
" We will then give our friends in North-
" Carolina _a fair trial._ If they behave like
" men, it may be of the greateſt advantage to
" the affairs of Britain. If they are as - - - -
" as our friends to the ſouthward, we muſt
" leave them to their fate, and _ſecure what we_
" _have got._" Had I not conſequently every
reaſon to expect his Lordſhip would have done
ſo? To what purpoſe then did his Lordſhip
march

march to Wilmington from Crofs-creek, as he was fo much nearer Camden and South Carolina? Or, even when at Wilmington, (as he could not but be apprehenfive for the fafety of South Carolina, from General Greene's march into that province; — and even for Charlestown,* *whofe old works were in part levelled, to* " *make way for new ones, which were not yet* " *conftructed; and whofe garrifon was inadequate* " *to oppofe any force of confequence;*" which material information it is prefumed Colonel Balfour could not have failed communicating to his Lordfhip as well as to Lord Rawdon,) why did not his Lordfhip retire to Charlestown by the route of Lockwood's folly and the Waggamaw? Which, it is the opinion of many others as well as mine, was practicable. For gallies might have fecured him the paffage of that river, and we then held the poft of George-town upon its banks: it was, moreover, early in the month of April, long before the droughts fet in, and it may therefore be prefumed there was not much danger of the mills wanting water, as his Lordfhip feems to

c 2 have

* Vide Lord Rawdon's Letter to Lord Cornwallis, dated May 24, 1781.

have apprehended.   Had his Lordſhip fortunately done ſo, South Carolina would have
been ſaved, and the fatal cataſtrophe which
afterwards happened to his army in the Cheſapeak avoided.   Lord Cornwallis in anſwer to
this ſays, " that he decided to march into
" Virginia, *as the ſafeſt and moſt effectual means*
" *of employing the ſmall corps under his command.*
" For the force in South Carolina was in his
" opinion ſufficient, when collected, to ſecure
" what was valuable to us in that province."
But his Lordſhip's letter to General Phillips,
of the 24th of April, (written a day or two
before he moved) ſo far from repreſenting this
march *as a ſafe one*, deſcribes it as moſt peri-
lous.   And if there was a poſſibility that his
Lordſhip's return to South Carolina (even by
ſea) might prevent any material part of that
province or Georgia from falling into the enemy's hands, (as many of the poſts there did,
notwithſtanding his Lordſhip's opinion of the
ſufficiency of the force to ſecure them,) it may be
preſumed, that his Lordſhip's *march into Vir-*
ginia was not the moſt effectual means of employing
the corps under his command, as the event has
but too well proved to our coſt.   Lord Cornwallis

wallis gives likewife another reafon for this move. He fays, " he was influenced by ha-
" ving juft received an account from Charles-
" town of the arrival of a frigate with dif-
" patches from me. The fubftance of which
" then tranfmitted to him was, that General
" Phillips had been detached to the Chefa-
" peak, and put under his orders. Which in-
" duced him *to hope that folid operations might*
" *be adopted in that quarter.*" I fhall therefore take the liberty of faying a few words on this paffage, which appears to me very neceffary to be explained.

The difpatches his Lordfhip alludes to, were my letters to his Lordfhip of the 2d, 5th, and 8th, of March, with a copy of my inftruc-tions to General Phillips. Captain Amherft, of the Sixtieth regiment, having charged him-felf with thofe of Lord Cornwallis, and other difpatches for Colonel Balfour, failed from New-York on the 20th of March, in a mer-chant fhip, called the Jupiter. And as Colo-nel Balfour acknowledged the receipt of them all, in his letter to me of the 7th of April, it is prefumable they were delivered to him on or before that day. This letter was brought to
me

me by his Majefty's fhip Amphitrite; which, having in her way called at Cape Fear, brought me a letter likewife from Lord Cornwallis, at Wilmington, dated the 10th of April. It is therefore to be lamented, that neither the difpatches themfelves, nor the fubftance of them, had been tranfmitted to his Lordfhip by that fhip. The Speedy packet too, which was fent from Charles-town foon after the Amphitrite, with letters to me of the 20th of April, called likewife in her way at Cape Fear, and brought me letters from his Lordfhip of the 22d, 23d, and 24th of April; but I am concerned to obferve, that fafe opportunity of conveying my difpatches to his Lordfhip was alfo mifled. Although Lord Cornwallis, in his letter to the American minifter of the 23d April, and in his introduction, intimates that the fubftance of thofe difpatches was fent to him on the 22d April; I fhould, notwithftanding, fuppofe, that what was fent to his Lordfhip as fuch muft have been improperly ftated. For by having recourfe to the difpatches at large, it will be feen, that fo far from *inducing his Lordfhip to hope that folid operation might be adopted in Virginia,*

3 (as

(as he intimates the fubftance of them did) it is prefumed, they would on the contrary have convinced him, that I had not even an idea of the fort (which, indeed, his Lordfhip might have already judged from my letter of 6th November) and therefore, inftead of influencing his Lordfhip's move into that province, they might have moft probably prevented it. But when the Public have read my letters to Lord Cornwallis of the 2d, 5th, and 8th of March, and my inftructions to General Phillips, they will be competent to judge in what manner they were moft likely to influence his Lordfhip, had he received them, or even the fubftance of them, before he commenced his march into Virginia, as I think his Lordfhip might have perceived by the *inftructions* that Generals Phillips and Arnold, with part of the Chefapeak corps, were to be drawn back to New-York for a particular fervice, after a certain time ; — and *by the letters*, that a confiderable French armament was failed from Rhode-ifland to the Chefapeak. It is confequently prefumable, that in the *firft inftance* his Lordfhip would not have marched into Virginia, *left he fhould interfere*

terfere with my plans; and that *in the other* he would have been equally cautious of doing fo, *left he fhould hazard the deftruction of his own corps*, fhould the troops in Chefapeak happen at the time to be invefted at Portf-mouth, which from thofe letters would appear very probable to be the cafe.

I will frankly own that I ever difapproved of an attempt to conquer Virginia before the Carolinas were abfolutely reftored. However, when I faw that Lord Cornwallis had forced himfelf upon me in that province, I left him at liberty to act there as he judged beft, as may appear by my letter to his Lordfhip of the 29th of May, which was the firft I had an opportunity of writing to him after my know-ledge of his arrival at Peterfburg, or of his intentions of coming here.

Although Lord Cornwallis thought proper to decline engaging in the plan of operations which I had propofed to him in cafe he had none of his own ; I am at a lofs to guefs what may be his motives for faying, " *I did not feem* " *inclined to take more fhare in the refponfibility* " *than barely to recommend it* ;" and indeed I cannot think his Lordfhip was really ferious

in

in fuggefting an infinuation fo apparently groundlefs. For it is manifeft that my letter to General Phillips of the 30th of April (pub-lifhed by Lord Cornwallis) conveys to him and General Arnold the *moft explicit inftructions* for carrying thofe operations into execution; and it can fcarcely be doubted, that thofe in-ftructions were equally *explicit to his Lordfhip*, the moment the command of that army de-volved upon him. Befides, though it may be admitted that I only *barely recommended* the move, in my letters on the fubject to his Lordfhip (becaufe it had been hitherto ufual for me to leave him to his own difcretion) yet I am perfuaded a reference to my corref-pondence (as publifhed by Lord Cornwallis and myfelf) will fhew that thofe recommen-dations were fufficiently explicit to fix re-fponfibility upon me, had his Lordfhip adopted my plan, and afterwards failed.

Lord Cornwallis is pleafed to fay, " that " he informed me he fhould repair to Wil-" liamiburg, about the time when he fhould " receive my anfwer, in order to be in readi-" nefs to execute my commands; and that he " fhould *employ the intermediate fpace* in de-

d   " ftroying

" ftroying fuch of the enemy's ftores and ma-
" gazines as might be within his reach."—
The letter which is thus explained was dated
the 26th of May, at Byrd's, a little more than
twenty miles from Richmond, which is fifty
from Williamſburg, and is expreffed in the
following words : " I ſhall *now* proceed to dif-
" lodge La Fayette *from Richmond,* and with
" my light troops to deftroy any magazines
" or ftores in the *neighbourhood,* which may
" have been collected either for his ufe or for
" General Greene's army. *From thence* I pur-
" pofe to move to the *Neck at Williamſburg,*
" which is reprefented as healthy, and keep
" myfelf unengaged from operations which
" might interfere with your plan for the cam-
" paign, until I have the fatisfaction of hear-
" ing from you. I hope I *ſhall then have an op-*
" *portunity to receive better information* than has
" hitherto been in my power to procure rela-
" tive to *a proper harbour and place of arms.*
" At prefent I am inclined to think well of
" York. *The objections to Portſmouth* are, *that*
" *it cannot be made ſtrong without an army to de-*
" *fend it, that it is remarkably unhealthy, and can*
" *give no protection to a ſhip of the line.*" From
the

the foregoing letter I naturally concluded, that, as foon as his Lordſhip had finiſhed the ſervice he was gone on, (which I did not imagine would have taken up above ſix or ſeven days at moſt) he would endeavour to *obtain information reſpecting a proper harbour and place of arms* ; and having found it, that he was actually employed in eſtabliſhing a poſt there. For, not having received any letter from his Lordſhip between the 26th of May and 30th of June, I was totally ignorant of his having changed his deſign, (as deſcribed in his letter of the firſt date) and *gone acroſs the country towards Frederickſburg, by Hanover Court-houſe* ; an operation which took his Lordſhip a complete month before he reached Williamſburg. But had his Lordſhip fortunately explained to me his inſtructions in that letter in the ſame manner he has now explained his letter, I ſhould have ſeen that his Lordſhip had no idea of eſtabliſhing a poſt on the Williamſburg Neck: and, when I found he had no plan of his own, would of courſe have ſent early and explicit orders for that purpoſe, either to his Lordſhip, or in his abſence to General Leſlie, whereby much time might have been ſaved,

and

and the fatal cataſtrophe that followed—at leaſt retarded, by his Lordſhip being in a better ſtate of defence than that in which the enemy found him. For, though from his Lordſhip's letter to me of the 22d of Auguſt*, I had every reaſon to ſuppoſe that a proper ſurvey of the ground had been taken, and a judicious plan fixed on for fortifying it; I very much fear that nothing material was done until after the arrival of the French fleet on the 29th of Auguſt, as the engineer has ſince given me to underſtand (when I aſked him for his ſurvey) that he did not take one. There appears, therefore, to have been a miſapprehenſion ſomewhere reſpecting this matter, as well as the number of intrenching tools; which, though computed by his Lordſhip† to be

* *Extract.—Letter from Lord Cornwallis to Sir H. Clinton, dated York-Town, Auguſt 22, 1781.*

" The engineer has *finiſhed his ſurvey* and examination " of *this place*, and has propoſed his plan for fortifying it; " which, appearing judicious, I have approved of, and " directed to be executed."

† *Extract.—Letter from Lord Cornwallis to Sir H. Clinton dated York-Town, October 20, 1781.*

" And our ſtock of intrenching tools, which *did not* " *much exceed four hundred,* when *we began to work* in the " latter end of Auguſt, was now much diminiſhed."

be only about four hundred when he began to
work on the York fide, I find by his engineer's
reports, in my poffeffion, to have been 992*
on the 23d of Auguft, the day on which (it
is prefumed from the letter before quoted) he
began to break ground.

Lord Cornwallis is alfo pleafed to fay,
" Whoever reads the correfpondence will fee,
" that fince Sir H. Clinton had declared pofi-
" tively in his firft, and in feveral fubfequent
" difpatches againft the plan for reducing
" Virginia, no *explicit alternative* was left to
" me, between complying with the requifition
" (contained in his letters of the 11th and
" 15th of June) of fuch troops as I could fpare
" from a healthy defenfive ftation, or engaging
" in operations in the Upper Chefapeak."
But this conclufion does not, I prefume ne-
ceffarily follow; for though it is admitted that
the whole of my correfpondence with the
American Minifter and Lord Cornwallis uni-
formly declare my fentiments, of the im-
practicability of reducing Virginia by an operation folely there, without the good-will and
aid of the inhabitants, — and of the bad policy
of

* Vide the return in the Appendix.

of the meafure from the unhealthinefs of the climate; and I was equally uniform in expreffing to his Lordfhip my wifhes, that he would adopt my ideas of the move to the Delaware Neck, &c. againft which there were none of thofe objections. Yet, when I found that his Lordfhip was averfe to engage in the operations concerted with General Phillips, and that he concurred with that officer refpecting the propriety of changing the poft of Portfmouth for one more healthy and defenfible, I gave my confent to the change propofed, and referred his Lordfhip to my correfpondence with General Phillips for my opinions thereon. His Lordfhip might have therefore judged that I expected he would immediately carry into execution this part of my plan, efpecially as his Lordfhip might have recollected that he told me in the letter before quoted, " That he hoped, when he got to the " Williamfburg Neck, he fhould have an op- " portunity to receive better information than " had hitherto been in his power to procure, " relative to a *proper harbour and place of* " *arms.*" Wherefore, as his Lordfhip was left at liberty by my letters of the 11th and

15th

15th of June, to detain all the troops, if he had not finished the operations he was engaged in : and as his Lordship had *not completed his measures relative to a proper harbour and place of arms*, which appears from his letter to have been one of the operations he proposed engaging in ; it may be fairly concluded that an *explicit alternative* was left him. For the letter of the 11th of June explicitly recommends to his Lordship *the taking a healthy defensive station* wherever he chose on the Williamsburg Neck ; and only calls for what troops he could spare from its ample defence and other purposes mentioned, *after it was taken.* And as his Lordship *had not yet taken that station*, the troops were without doubt to be detained ;— because *in that case only* my letter requested them to be sent; but though his Lordship might possibly have understood the letter differently at the time, we may at least suppose that, as it referred him to other letters of the 29th of May and 8th of June, for a further explanation of my wishes, and these letters had not then been received by his Lordship, he had very sufficient reason *to suspend at least* his intention of crossing James River, until

4   he

he either received them or heard again from
New-York. Lord Cornwallis endeavours to
invalidate this reasoning by saying, " that the
" choice of a healthy station was controlled
" by other material confiderations, particularly
" the *imminent danger of New-York*, and the *im-*
" *portant effects expected from the expedition*
" *against Philidelphia.*" His Lordship will,
however, forgive me if I cannot difcover
from whence those confiderations arofe ; as my
letters of the 11th and 15th of June (which
were the only letters *he had *then* received) do
not defcribe New-York to *be in any fort of
danger*, and his Lordship by his anfwer to
thofe letters feemed of opinion, *that the project against Philadelphia was then become inexpedient*. I am therefore forry to be under the
neceffity of repeating, that it is my opinion,
his Lordship totally mifonceived all my orders
and intentions refpecting this bufinefs, when
he judged they warranted his *paffing James
River* and retiring to *Portfmouth* ; — *which* I
could not poffibly fufpect his Lordship would
make choice of as a *healthy defenfible station*,
                                                    after

---

* **Vide his Lordship's** letter of the 30th of June.

after he had juſt told me in his letter of the
26th of May, " that it was *remarkably un-*
" *healthy, and (though fortified) required an*
" *army to defend it.*"   But our correſpondence
is now before the public, and they will judge
whether my orders authorized his Lordſhip to
do ſo, and whether conſequently ſix weeks at
leaſt were not loſt *in ſecuring a place of arms,*
which we both ſeemed to concur in opinion
was neceſſary.   With reſpect to his Lordſhip's
ſaying, " It will be ſeen by the correſpondence
" that the Commander-in-chief's opinion of
" the indiſpenſible neceſſity of a harbour for
" line of battle ſhips only appears in his letter
" of the 11th of July, after he had been ac-
" quainted that the troops intended for the
" expedition againſt Philadelphia would be
" ſoon ready to ſail," (thereby intimating that
it was a new idea juſt then ſtarted) I preſume
it may be eaſily made appear from the ſame
correſpondence, that ſo far from being a new
idea, *the taking a ſtation for large ſhips* was one
of the earlieſt and principal objects recommended to General Phillips's conſideration and
enquiry.*   And I think it may be inferred,
e   from

* Vide inſtructions of the 10th of March.

from his Lordſhip's objecting to Portſmouth, in the letter of the 26th of May, " *becauſe it* " *could not give protection to a ſhip of the line,*" that he regarded it as ſuch, and conſequently went in ſearch of a naval ſtation *as ſtanding in that general officer's place*, it being apparently from that letter one of the principal reaſons which induced his Lordſhip to go to the Williamſburg Neck.

Lord Cornwallis ſays, " Hampton-road was " recommended by that order; but as it was " upon examination found totally unfit for the " purpoſe deſired, every perſon can judge *whe-* " *ther the order did not then in its ſpirit become* " *poſitive to occupy York and Glouceſter.*" To enable every perſon therefore to judge whether it did or not, I ſhall beg leave to tranſcribe the words of the order. " I requeſt that your Lord- " ſhip will without loſs of time *examine Old Point* " *Comfort, and fortify it.* But if it ſhould be " your Lordſhip's opinion that Old Point " Comfort *cannot be held without having poſſeſſion* " *of York*, for *in this caſe* Glouceſter may per- " haps be not ſo material) *and that the whole* " cannot be done with leſs than ſeven thouſand " men, you are at full liberty to detain all the " troops

" troops now in Chefapeak, which I believe
" amount to fomewhat more than that num-
" ber. Which very liberal conceffion will, I
" am perfuaded, convince your Lordfhip of
" the high eftimation in which I hold a naval
" ftation in Chefapeak." If nothing elfe had
been faid to Lord Cornwallis or General Phillips, upon the fubject of a naval ftation, but
what this order contains; there could not in
my humble opinion be a doubt, that his Lordfhip was not at liberty to take any other than
Old Point Comfort, — except he fhould be of
opinion that *York was neceffary to cover it, in
which cafe he might take York alfo*; and as the
two pofts might probably require more troops
than were intended to be left in Chefapeak, his
Lordfhip was at liberty to detain the whole *for
fortifying and garrifoning* them. I dare fay Lord
Cornwallis faw the order in this point of view;--
but judging that Old Point Comfort was totally
unfit for the purpofe defired, he had recourfe
to the inftructions and letters to General Phillips in his poffeffion, to fee whether they would
authorife him to reject it, and look out for
another. And difcovering that my inftructions
to that General officer gave him leave, " in

" cafe

" cafe the Admiral difapproving Portfmouth
" fhould require a fortified ftation for large
" fhips in Chefapeak, and *fhould propofe York*
" *town or Old Point Comfort*, to take poffeffion
" thereof, if poffeffion of either could be *ac-*
" *quired and maintained without great rifk or*
" *lofs* ;" his Lordfhip conceived he fhould aft
according to the fpirit of my orders, by taking
York and Gloucefter. I am however humbly
of opinion, that admitting the propriety of his
Lordfhip's confulting other papers befides the
order immediately before him, the order (even
as explained by the inftructions) did not *become*
pofitive to occupy York and Gloucefter. For it does
not appear that the inftructions authorifed either
General Phillips or his Lordfhip to occupy
York or Old Point Comfort, *unlefs they fhould*
have been propofed by the Admiral for a naval
fiation. But the poft of York and Gloucefter
never having been propofed by the Admiral
either to his Lordfhip or me for a naval ftation,
as Old Point Comfort was, but only barely
mentioned to his Lordfhip by the Admiral, as
likely to command one of the principal rivers
if it could be fecured ; and it at laft appearing by
the letter of 20th October, to have been his

Lordfhip's

Lordſhip's opinion that it was *incapable of being
ſo* ; it may be preſumed that his Lordſhip did
not act conformable to either the ſpirit or letter
of the order in taking it, — and conſequently
that his *doing ſo was entirely of his own motion
and choice*. But, being probably aware of this
concluſion, his Lordſhip ſays, " as the harbour
" was the indiſpenſible object, he took York,
" being the only one in Cheſapeak that he knew
" of." In which (no doubt) his Lordſhip
would have been perfectly juſtifiable *if the objections to it were not ſuch as he thought forcible.*"
But it appears from his Lordſhip's letter of the
20th of October, *that the objections to that poſt
were ſuch as he thought forcible.* It may therefore be a matter of ſome ſurpriſe, that, as his
Lordſhip thought proper to avail himſelf of the
latitude of choice he ſuppoſed given him by the
inſtructions to General Phillips, it did not occur to him that the ſame inſtructions directed
him to " *decline taking either York or Old Point
" Comfort, if his objections were ſuch as he
" thought forcible.*" And as Lord Cornwallis
never ſtated his objections to the poſt of York either
to the Admiral or me, as thoſe inſtructions
directed him to do, if he had any ; it may be
aſſerted

afferted that his Lordſhip alone is anſwerable for whatever impropriety there may have been in *taking the poſt of York and Glouceſter* ; as it is I preſume, clear from the foregoing reaſoning, that, having under the ſanction of the inſtructions to General Phillips, declined taking poſſeſſion of *Old Point Comfort* (which his Lordſhip was poſitively directed to occupy by the order of the 11th of July,) his Lordſhip had *the ſame authority for declining to take York or any other naval ſtation,* " could they not " be *acquired and maintained without great riſk* " *or loſs, and ſo well and ſo ſoon fortified as to be* " *rendered hors d' inſulte before the enemy could* " *move a force, &c. againſt them ;*"* which his Lordſhip's letter of the 20th of October intimates to be his opinion the poſt of York could not be *from the diſadvantageous nature of the ground.*

Having repreſented to the miniſter for the American department the danger of operations in Cheſapeak without a covering fleet ; and having been in conſequence promiſed that I ſhould have it ; and being told by Admiral

---

* Vide the inſtructions and ſubſtance of converſations with General Phillips ; as quoted by Lord Cornwallis in his letter dated July 26, 1781.

ral Hood upon his arrival that he had brought me a fufficient one; I gave Lord Cornwallis of courfe all the hopes I could, and " *certain-* " *ly promifed to fuccour him in perfon, by moving* " *into Chefapeak with four thoufand troops,*" the inftant the Admiral fhould inform me the paf-fage to him was open, or would undertake to convoy me. But as his Lordfhip did not re-ceive thefe hopes (fuch as they are) before the 16th of September; (for I muft ftill perfift in declaring that I never gave his Lordfhip *affu-rances of the exertions of the navy* before my let-ter to him of the 24th of September, which he received on the 29th — as afferted in his Lord-fhip's letter of the 20th of October) Surely his Lordfhip's hopes of fuccour muft have been but fmall between the 29th of Auguft and that pe-riod, *when he knew there was an enemy's fleet of thirty-fix fail of the line blocking him up, and a formidable army collecting to inveft him,* " in an " intrenched camp, fubject in moft places to " enfilade, and the ground in general difad- " vantageous ;" — without *knowing of more than feven fail of the line on our fide,* and confe-quently having in the intermediate fpace no very great profpect of relief.

His

His Lordſhip ſays, " that, as I did not give
" him the ſmalleſt particle of diſcretionary
" power different from holding the poſts he
" occupied ; it would not have been juſtifiable
" in him, either to abandon by the evacuation
" of York a conſiderably quantity of artillery,
" the ſhips of war, tranſports, proviſions,
" ſtores, and hoſpitals ; or, by venturing an
" action without the moſt manifeſt advantage,
" to run the riſk of precipitating the loſs of
" them." To this, I ſhall only obſerve, that
it will appear from the correſpondence, that his
Lordſhip's diſcretionary powers were unlimited
from the firſt moment of his taking charge of
a ſeparate command ; and it will I believe be
admitted, that his Lordſhip acted in moſt
caſes as if he conſidered them as ſuch. And
though I may not condemn his Lordſhip for
not attacking the Marquis de la Fayette, before
his junction with Monſieur St. Simon (when
he had, as I underſtand, only two thouſand
regular continental troops); or for not at-
tempting to prevent that junction ; or for not
attacking them when joined ; and endeavouring to eſcape with part of his army to the ſouthward, between the 29th of Auguſt and the
16th

16th of September; — as fuch meafures muft.
have altogether depended on his Lordfhip's
own feelings, of which no man can fpeak but
himfelf. Yet it was natural to fuppofe, that
the General officer, who had but a few months
before (at the rifk of engaging his Commander
in Chief in operations, for which he could not
be prepared; and perhaps at the rifk of lofing
a valuable province under his immediate protection) decided upon a move with part of his
army into Virginia, *" for urgent reafons,"*
" being influenced thereto (he fays) *by the fubftance of a difpatch,* (he heard was coming to
him,) without waiting to receive it, though
it might have been expected in a few hours : —
I fay, it was natural to fuppofe, that the General officer who had done this, might have
judged it equally expedient to decide upon retiring back again without waiting to receive
fpecial difcretionary powers from his Commander,
in Chief, if he judged there was a great probability of his lofing every thing fhould he
remain. Which, if it was fo, I am bold to
fay, was a reafon far more urgent for his endeavouring to fave part of his army by any
means in his power, than any his Lordfhip

f   could

could fuppofe he had for quitting the Carolinas
at the time he marched into Virginia.

There remains little more neceflary in reply
to Lord Cornwallis's introduction, but to obferve, that the army and its followers in Virginia had been fo increafed in confequence of his
Lordfhip's move into that province ; that it
would have been impracticable to withdraw
them by water (as his Lordfhip is pleafed to
fuggeft) for want of tranfports, even if the
American minifter had not directed me to fupport his Lorfhip there, and a preffing contin-
gency had required it. And I muft take the
liberty to fay, that the fending his Lordfhip's
corps back to South Carolina by land, would
have been a moft abfurd idea for me to adopt
after the opinions I had given of the rifks it
run in its former march by that route.

I fhall now beg leave to conclude with an
opinion, which I prefume is deducible from
the foregoing (I truft candid) review of circumftances. Which is, that Lord Cornwallis's
conduct and opinions, if they were not the
immediate caufes, may be adjudged to have at
leaft contributed to bring on the fatal cataf-
trophe

trophe which terminated the unfortunate campaign of 1781.

H. CLINTON.

Harley - Street,
    April 3, 1783.

A P P E N D I X.

P A R T   I.

CONTAINING

E X T R A C T S

FROM THE

Correspondence with Earl Cornwallis, respecting the Force left with his Lordship, and the Instructions given him upon his taking the Command of the Southern District.

Extract. — From Sir Henry Clinton to Earl Corn-wallis, dated Charles-town, May 17, 1780.

YOUR Lordship has already with you, *(in the field)* two thousand five hundred and forty two rank and file; but, if you have the least reason to suppose the enemy likely to be in great number, you shall be reinforced with the forty-second, the light infantry, and any other corps you choose. As your move is important, it must not be stinted. —I will give you all you wish of every sort. —

B   Let

Let me but know what it is as foon as poffible. In the mean time, I fhall order the light infantry and forty-fecond regiment to prepare; depending upon it, that as foon as you can fpare them, you will return them to me; for all operations to the Northward muft be cramped without them. If you choofe to keep the feventeenth dragoons, you are heartily welcome to them during this move.

Copy. — From Earl Cornwallis to Sir Henry Clinton, dated Camp at Manigolds, May 18, 1780.

SIR,

LIEUTENANT Colonel Webfter arrived this morning, and informed me of the meffage which you fent by him, relative to reinforcing the corps under my command. The fervice on which I am going, is undoubtedly of the moft important nature, and in my opinion, without fome fuccefs in the back country, our fuccefs at Charles-town would but little promote the real interefts of Great-Britain. But at the fame time it is as neceffary that your fituation to the Northward fhould be re-fpeĉtable. It would be with great regret that I fhould fee you leave behind any part of that corps deftined for your firft embarkation. The garrifon, then,

then, of Charles-town and Sullivan's-ifland, will confift of three Britifh regiments, — two of them very weak, — and two Heffian, and one weak Provincial, the latter of which, perhaps, will be fent to Fort Moultrie. This garrifon will have the charge of two thoufand five hundred prifoners. The corps at prefent under my command is, in my opinion, fully equal to the purpofe intended by it, unlefs fome confiderable reinforcement of Continentals fhould come from the Northward. I have not yet heard that fact afcertained, by any intelligence which has come to my knowledge. If troops are on their march, and not very near, your embarkation given out publicly for the Chefapeak will probably ftop them. I think, therefore, Sir, if you pleafe, with proper deference and fubmiffion to your opinion, that the bufinefs may be fettled in the following manner: If no certain intelligence arrives before you are ready to fail, of a confiderable corps of the Continental troops being far advanced, that the difpofition fhould then remain the fame which you mentioned when I had the honour of feeing you. If fuch intelligence fhould arrive before that time, I fhould then wifh to be joined by five or fix hundred men, either Britifh or Heffian, and fubmit it to your judgment on the fpot, from whence they could be beft fupplied. I think, at all events, Lieutenant-colonel Balfour's expedition fhould go on immediately, as the feafon

of

of the year makes it neceffary that he fhould lofe no time. The more pains that can be taken to eftablifh the belief of your going to Virginia, the greater will be the probability of ftopping their reinforcement.

I am, &c.

(Signed)   CORNWALLIS.

———————

Extract. — From Earl Cornwallis to Sir Henry Clinton, dated Camp at Manigolds, May 19, 1780.

S I R,

I RECEIVED, very early this morning, the favour of your letter by Lieutenant-colonel Innes, to which the letter I had the honour of fending to you yefterday, by Major Danfey, will ferve as an anfwer. I can only add, that I have received no intelligence whatever of reinforcements coming to the enemy from the Northward, or of their being in force in this province.

Extract.

Extract. — *From Sir Henry Clinton to Earl Corn-wallis, dated Charles-town, May* 20, 1780.

———— T H E light infantry and forty-fecond regiment march this evening to Goofe-creek, and thence to Monk's-corner, where they will remain at your Lordfhip's call, in readinefs either to join you, or to return and embark, as fhall have become expedient.

———————————

Extract. — *From Sir Henry Clinton to Earl Corn-wallis, dated Charles-town, May* 20, 1780.

EVERY jealoufy has been and will be given on my part, as a blind to our real intentions.

And now, my Lord, having entered into every thing that occurs to me as neceffary to be thought on at prefent, I heartily wifh fuccefs to your important move. I cannot doubt your having it, for as much as I agree with you, that fuccefs at Charles-town, unlefs followed in the back country, will be of little avail; fo much, I am perfuaded, that the taking that place in the advantageous manner we have done it, infures the reduction of this and the next province, if the temper of our friends in thofe diftricts is fuch as it has always been reprefented to us.

I

Extract.

Extract. — From Earl Cornwallis to Sir Henry Clinton, dated Camp at Lenews, East Side of Santée, May 21, 1780.

THE march of the light infantry and forty-second to Monk's-corner will be of use to those corps, and will help to spread alarm through the country ; but from what I hear, I do not believe that there can be any necessity for detaining any part of the first embarkation a moment after the ships are ready for them.

Extract. — Sir Henry Clinton to Earl Cornwallis, dated Charles-Town, June 1, 1780.

WE shall probably leave this in a day or two. — I dare not be so sanguine as to suppose that your business will be compleated in time for us to meet before I sail; and as our communication will become precarious, I think it necessary to give your Lordship outlines of my intentions, where your Lordship is likely to bear a part. Your Lordship knows it was part of my plan to have gone into Chesapeak bay ; but I am apprehensive the information which the Admiral and I received, may make it necessary for him to assemble his fleet at New-York,

in

—in which cafe I fhall go there likewife. When your Lordfhip has finifhed your campaign, you will be better able to judge what is neceffary to be done to fecure South and recover North Carolina. Perhaps it may be neceffary to fend the gallies and fome troops into Cape Fear, to awe the lower counties, by far the moft hoftile of that province, and to prevent the conveyance of fuccours by inland navigation, the only communication that will probably remain with the northern parts of North Carolina and Virginia. Should your Lordfhip fo far fucceed in both provinces, as to be fatisfied they are fafe from any attack during the approaching feafon, after leaving a fufficient force in garrifon, and fuch other pofts as you think neceffary, and fuch troops by way of moving corps as you fhall think fufficient, added to fuch provincial and militia corps as you fhall judge proper to raife ; I fhould wifh you to affift in operations which will certainly be carried on in the Chefapeak, as foon as we are relieved from our apprehenfion of a fuperior fleet, and the feafon will admit of it in that climate. This may happen, perhaps, about September, or, if not, early in October. I am clear this fhould not be atttempted without a great naval force ; — I am not fo clear there fhould be a great land force. I therefore propofe that your Lordfhip, with what you can fpare at the time from your important poft, *(which is always to be confidered as the principal object)* may meet the Admiral,

who

who will bring with him such additional force as I can spare into the Chesapeak. I should recommend in the first place, that one or two armed ships, vigilants, should be prepared, and that as many gallies as can go to sea may likewise accompany you from hence. Our first object will probably be the taking post at Norfolk or Suffolk, *or near the Hampton Road,* and then proceeding up the Chesapeak to *Baltimore.* I shall not presume to say any thing by way of instruction to your Lordship, except in articles where you wish it; and if you will do me the honour to inform me of your wishes by the first safe opportunity, I shall pay every attention to them upon that subject, or any other. The Admiral assures me that there will be ships enough left for convoy, ready by the 24th of June. Your Lordship will be the best judge what use can be made of them. Correspondence may, and I hope will, be kept up by the cruizers, which the Admiral and officer stationed here will have, but if you find it necessary, you will be so good to press or hire armed vessels.

Extract. — From Instructions to Lieutenant-General Earl Cornwallis, dated Head-Quarters, Charlestown, June 1, 1780.

UPON my departure from hence, you will be pleased to take command of the troops mentioned in the

the inclofed return, and of all other troops now here, or that may arrive in my abfence. Your Lordfhip will make fuch change in the pofition of them, as you may judge moft conducive to his Majefty's fervice, for the defence of this important poft, and its dependencies. At the fame time, it is by no means my intention to prevent your acting offenfively, in cafe an opportunity fhould offer, confiftent with the *fecurity of this place*, which is always to be regarded as *a primary object*.

All provifion and military ftores of any denomination now here, or which may hereafter arrive, are fubmitted to your Lordfhip's orders, together with every power you may find neceffary to enforce in my abfence, for the promotion of the King's fervice.

Extract.—From Sir Henry Clinton to Earl Cornwalllis, dated Romulus, June 8, 1780.

MY LORD,

I HAVE the honour to tranfmit to your Lordfhip the names of feveral inhabitants of the town, who figned an addrefs, the copy of which Brigadier-general Paterfon will fend you. Inclofed is a copy of the anfwer the Admiral propofed fending until I reprefented to him that the fubfcribers were un-

C   known

known to us as to their feveral characters; that the fuperintendant was not with us to be confulted; that the permitting exportation amounted to opening the port, which we were not empowered to do; and that I would, reluctantly, at the hour of my departure, change, within your Lordfhip's command, the conditions of fo many perfons, without knowing their merits. I alfo confidered that property, in the late troubles, might have been very unwarrantably acquired, and that exportation realized it to the prefent poffeffors.

In confequence, the inclofed anfwer was fubftituted, bettering their prefent condition, and opening the profpect of trade, and the reftoration of civil government.

To this, my Lord, I have to add, in the Admiral's and my own name, that you are empowered ftill farther to indulge men who exhibit proofs of a fincere return to their duty, by admitting them to any greater degree of liberty, to the fulleft enjoyment of their property, and to the permiffion, in particular cafes, of fhipping it, when the officer commanding the King's fhips fhall furnifh convoy; all which advantages I will ratify either as Commiffioner or Commander-in-chief.

PART II.

PART II.

Copies and Extracts from Letters, relative to the entire Submiffion of South Carolina, and the progreffive Operations propofed in Confequence, for the Reduction of North Carolina.

———————

Extract. — From Earl Cornwallis to Sir Henry Clinton, dated Charles-town, June 30, 1780.

——THE fubmiffion of General Williamfon at Ninety-Six, whofe capitulation I inclofe with Captain Paris's letter; and the difperfion of a party of rebels, who had affembled at an Iron-work, on the north weft border of the province, by a detachment of dragoons and militia, from Lieutenant-colonel Turnbull, put an end to all refiftance in South Carolina.

FROM THE SAME.

THE force of the enemy in North Carolina confits of about one hundred militia at Crofs-Creek, under General Cafwell; four or five hundred militia, at or near Salifbury, under General Rutherford; and three hundred Virginians in that neighbourhood, under one Porterfield.

———— returned with information that he faw two thoufand Maryland and Delaware troops at Hillfborough under Major-general De Calbe. Other accounts correfponded with his. But I have fince heard that the greateft part of the laft have returned to Virginia.

After having thus fully ftated the prefent fituation of the two Carolinas, I fhall now take the liberty of giving my opinion, with refpect to the practicability and the probable effect of farther operations in this quarter, and my own intentions, if not otherwife directed by your Excellency. I think, that with the force at prefent under my command (except there fhould be a confiderable *foreign* interference) I can leave South Carolina in fecurity, and march about the beginning of September, with a body of troops, into the back part of North Carolina, with the greateft probability of reducing that province to its duty. And if this be accomplifhed, I am of opinion, that (befides the advantage of poffeffing fo valuable a province)

vince)

vince) it would prove an effectual barrier for South Carolina and Georgia; and could be kept, with the affistance of our friends there, by as few troops as would be wanted on the borders of this province, if North Carolina fhould remain in the hands of our enemies. Confequently, if your Excellency fhould continue to think it expedient to employ part of the troops at prefent in this province, in operations in the Chefapeak, there will be as many to fpare, as if we did not poffefs North Carolina. If I am not honoured with different directions from your Excellency before that time, I fhall take my meafures for beginning the execution of the above plan about the latter end of Auguft, or beginning of September, and fhall apply to the officer commanding his Majefty's fhips for fome co-operation, by Cape Fear, which at prefent would be burthenfome to the navy, and not of much importance to the fervice.

Extract. — *From Earl Cornwallis to Sir Henry Clinton, dated Charles-town, July,* 14, 1780.

I HAVE the fatisfaction to affure your Excellency, that the numbers and difpofitions of our militia, equal my moft fanguine expectations. But ftill I muft confefs, that their want of fubordination and confi-

confidence in themfelves, will make a confiderable regular force always neceffary for the defence of the province, until North Carolina is perfectly reduced. It will be needlefs to attempt to take any confiderable number of the South Carolina militia with us, when we advance. They can only be looked upon as light troops, and we fhall find friends enough in the next province of the fame quality; and we muft not undertake to fupply too many ufelefs mouths.

———————

Extract. — From Earl Cornwallis to Sir Henry Clinton, dated Charles-town, Aug. 6, 1780.

S I R,

I RECEIVED by Major England, your letters of the 14th and 15th of July; and am very glad to find by the latter, that you do not place much dependance on receiving troops from hence.

My letter of the 14th, by the Halifax, will have convinced you of the impoffibility of weakening the force in this province; and every thing which has happened fince that time, tends more ftrongly to confirm it. The general ftate of things in the two provinces of North and South Carolina, is not very materially altered fince my letters of the 14th and 15th of laft month were written.   Frequent

4   fkirmifhes,

fkirmifhes, with various fuccefs, have happened in the country between the Catawba-river and Broad-river. The militia of the diftrict about Tiger and Ennoree rivers, was formed by us, under a Colonel Floyd; Colonel Neale, the rebel colonel, had fled; but Lieutenant-colonel Lifle, who had been paroled to the iflands, exchanged, on his arrival in Charles-town, his parole for a certificate of his being a good fubject, returned to the country, and carried off the whole battalion to join General Sumpter, at Catawba. We have not, however, on the whole, loft ground in that part of the country. Turnbull was attacked at Rocky-mount, by Sumpter, with about twelve hundred men, militia and refugees, from this province, whom he repulfed with great lofs. We had on our part, an officer killed, and one wounded, and about ten or twelve men killed and wounded. Colonel Turnbull's conduct was very meritorious. The affair of Captain Huck turned out of lefs con-fequence than it appeared at firft; the Captain and three men of the legion were killed, and feven men of the New-York volunteers taken.

On the eaftern part of the province, we have been more unfortunate. By this time the reports induftri-oufly propagated in this province, of a large army coming from the northward, had very much inti-midated our friends, encouraged our enemies, and determined the wavering againft us; to which

our

our not advancing and acting offensively likewise contributed.

The whole country between Pedée and Santée has ever since been in an absolute state of rebellion; every friend of Government has been carried off, and his plantation destroyed; and detachments of the enemy have appeared on the Santée, and threatened our stores and convoys on that river. I have not heard that they have as yet made any attempt on them; and I hope, by this time, the steps I have taken will secure them. This unfortuate business, if it should have no worse consequences, will shake the confidence of our friends in this province, and make our situation very uneasy until we can advance. The wheat harvest in North Carolina is now over, but the weather is still excessively hot, and notwithstanding our utmost exertions, a great part of the rum, salt, clothing, and necessaries for the soldiers, and the arms for the Provincials and ammunition for the troops, are not far advanced on their way to Camden. However, if no material interruption happens, this business will be nearly accomplished in a fortnight or three weeks. It may be doubted by some, whether the invasion of North Carolina may be a prudent measure; but I am convinced it is a necessary one, and that if we do not attack that province, we must give up both South Carolina and Georgia, and retire within the walls of Charles-town. Our assurances of attachment

ment from our poor diftreffed friends in North Carolina are as ftrong as ever, and the patience and
fortitude with which thofe unhappy people bear
the moft oppreffive and cruel tyranny, that ever was
exercifed over any country, deferve our greateft ad-
miration. The Highlanders have offered to form a
regiment as foon as we enter the country, and
have defired that Governor Martin may be their
chief. I have confented with the rank of Lieutenant-
colonel commandant; the men they affure us are
already engaged.

· · An early diverfion in my favour in Chefapeak Bay,
will be of the greateft and moft important advantage
to my operations. I moft earneftly hope that the
admiral will be able to fpare a convoy for that purpofe.

I propofe taking the following corps with me into
North Carolina, twenty-third, thirty-third, fixty-
third, feventy-firft, volunteers of Ireland, Hamil-
ton's, Harrifon's, new-raifed, legion cavalry, and
infantry, North Carolina refugees. I intend to leave
on the frontiers, from Pedée to Waxhaw (to awe the
diffaffected, who, I am forry to fay, are ftill very
numerous in that country, and to prevent any infurrection in our rear) the New York volunteers, and
Brown's corps, and fome of the militia of the Camden diftrict, who are commanded by Colonel Rugely,
a very active and fpirited man. I fhall place Fergufon's corps and fome militia of the Ninety-fix diftrict,

D   which

which Colonel Balfour affures me are got into very tolerable order, owing to the great affiduity of Fergufon, on the borders of Tryon county, with directions for him to advance with a part of them into the mountains, and fecure the left of our march. Lieutenant-colonel Cruger, who commands at Ninety-fix, will have his own corps, Innes's and the remainder of the militia of that diftrict, to preferve that frontier, which requires great attention, and where there are many diffaffected, and many conftantly in arms. Allen's corps, and for a time, the Florida rangers, are ftationed at Augufta, under the command of Lieunant-colonel Allen.

———— I have already explained the meafures I had taken for eftablifhing a government, and fecuring this country by means of a militia. I have likewife paid as much attention as poffible to the civil and commercial matters. The principal objects of my attention will appear in the five proclamations, which I have iffued, and which I have the honour of inclofing to your Excellency.

I have the honour, &c.

(Signed)   CORNWALLIS.

PAT III.

PART III.

CONTAINING

EXTRACTS

FROM THE

Correfpondence with Earl Cornwallis, refpecting the Events which occurred between the Battle of Camden and Major Fergufon's Defeat.

———————

Extract. — From Earl Cornwallis to Sir Henry Clinton, dated Camden, August 23, 1780.

I HAVE not yet heard any accounts from North Carolina; but I hope that our friends will immediately take arms, as I have directed them to do. The diverfion in the Chefapeak will be of the utmoft importance. The troops here have gained reputation, but they have loft numbers; and there can be no doubt but the enemy will ufe every effort to repel an attack, which, if fuccefsful, muft end in their lofing all the Southern Colonies.

I have likewife to obferve, that if a general exchange fhould take place, the enemy's prifoners fhould, in my opinion, be delivered at the fame place as ours are fent to.

It

It is difficult to form a plan of operations, which must depend so much on circumstances. But it at present appears to me that I should endeavour to get as soon as possible to Hillsborough, and there assemble and try to arrange the friends who are inclined to arm in our favour; and endeavour to form a very large magazine for the winter, of flour and meal from the country; and of rum, salt, &c. from Cross-creek, which I understand to be about eighty miles carriage. But all this will depend on the operations which your Excellency may think proper to pursue in the Chesapeak, which appears to me next to the security of New-York, to be one of the most important objects of the war. I can only repeat what I have often had the honour of saying to you, that wherever you may think my presence can be most conducive to the good of his Majesty's service, thither I am at all times ready and willing to go.

Extract. — *From Earl Cornwallis to Lord George Germain, dated Camden, August 20, 1780.*

IN the district of ninety-six, by far the most populous and powerful of the province, Lieutenant-colonel Balfour by his great attention and diligence, and by the active assistance of Major Fergufon, who was appointed Inspector-general of militia of this province by Sir Henry Clinton, had formed seven battalions of militia, consisting of above four thousand men, and entirely composed of persons well-affected

affected to the Britiſh Government; which were ſo regulated that they could with eaſe furniſh fifteen hundred men at a ſhort notice, for the defence of the frontier, or any other home ſervice. But I muſt take this opportunity of obſerving, that this militia can be of little uſe for diſtant operations, as they will not ſtir without a horſe, and on that account your Lordſhip will eaſily conceive the impoſſibility of keeping a number of them together without deſtroying the country.

Extract. — From Earl Cornwallis to Lord George Germain, dated Camden, Auguſt 21, 1780.

ON the morning of the 17th I diſpatched proper people into North-Carolina, with directions to our friends there to take arms and aſſemble immediately; and to ſeize the moſt violent people and all military ſtores and magazines belonging to the rebels, and to intercept all ſtragglers from the routed army. And I have promiſed to march without loſs of time to their ſupport. Some neceſſary ſupplies for the army are now on their way from Charles-town; and I hope that their arrival will enable me to move in a few days.

Extract. — From Earl Cornwallis to Sir Henry Clinton, dated Camden, Auguſt 29, 1780.

I HOPE to be able to move my firſt diviſion in eight or nine days into North Carolina by Charlotte-town

town and Salifbury; the fecond will follow in about ten days after, with convalefcents and ftores. I fhall leave the New York volunteers and Innes's corps to take care of this place until the fick and ftores can be removed. Our ficknefs at prefent is rather at a ftand, the recoveries nearly keeping pace with the falling down. I dread the convalefcents not being able to march; but it is very tempting to try it, as a move of forty or fifty miles would put us into a much better climate.

Fergufon is to move into Tryon County with fome militia, whom he fays he is fure *he can depend upon for doing their duty and fighting well*; *but I am forry to fay that his own experience as well as that of every other officer is againft him.*

I moft fincerely hope that nothing can happen to prevent your Excellency's intended diverfion in the Chefapeak. If unfortunately any unforefeen caufe fhould make it impoffible, I fhould hope that you will fee the abfolute neceffity of adding fome force to the Carolinas.

Extract. — From Sir Henry Clinton to Earl Cornwallis, dated New-York, September 20, 1780.

I HAVE always thought operation in the Chefapeak of the greateft importance, and have often mentioned to Admiral Arbuthnot the neceffity of making a diverfion in your Lordfhip's favour in that

quarter

quarter; but have not been able till now to obtain a convoy for this purpose.

Your Lordship will receive inclosed a sketch of the instructions I intend to give to Major-general Leslie, who will command the expedition; which will give a general idea of the design of the move. But if your Lordship should wish any particular co-operation from that armament, General Leslie will of course consider himself under your Lordship's orders, and pay every obedience thereto.

I have the honour to inclose the copy of a letter I wrote to Lord George Germain, and of his Lordship's answer, respecting the option Lord Rawdon had made in favour of his provincial rank. And I am happy in having it in my power to communicate to his Lordship the King's pleasure that he should still retain his rank of Lieutenant-colonel in the line, which I beg leave to take this opportunity of doing through your Lordship.

INCLOSURES.

Copy.— *Sir Henry Clinton to Lord George Germain, dated Charles-Town, June 3, 1780.*

MY LORD,

LORD Rawdon, in consequence of his Majesty's order signified to me by your Lordship, has resigned his commission of Lieutenant-colonel in the army, and made choice of that of Colonel of Provincias

In

In justice to his Lordship, as well as to the King's service, I must observe that the expences Lord Rawdon has been at, and the distinguished zeal he has shewn in forming the corps under his command, render him worthy of much commendation, and make the alternative put to him a very mortifying one; whilst on the other hand, the volunteers of Ireland, bereft of a chief of his Lordship's rank in life, and attention to the service, would probably have lost much in their strength and discipline.

Perhaps his Majesty may be graciously pleased to consider his Lordship in the light of an officer, who, for the good of his service and the preservation of a serviceable corps, to which he felt a kind of parental attachment, has offered to relinquish rank essential to his future hopes as a soldier; and may, in consequence, restore to him his brevet of Lieutenant-colonel in the army.

I have the honour, &c.

H. CLINTON.

Extract. — From Lord G. Germain to Sir H. Clinton, dated Whitehall, July 5, 1780.

You will find by my separate letter of yesterday, that it is not his Majesty's intention to confine you to so strict an observance of the general rule of no officers being permitted to hold commissions in a regular and provincial corps at the same time, as to

prevent

prevent you from deviating from it in extraordinary cafes; and that your having done fo in favour of Majors Simcoe and Tarleton, was approved by his Majefty. I alfo informed you, that the general rule was not meant to affect the brevet rank of officers. It is therefore a great concern to me to find Lord Rawdon had refigned his rank of Lieutenant-colonel in the army, when he made his option of Colonel of the Provincials. The King is fully fenfible of his Lordfhip's merit, and of the great advantage which the corps under his command has derived from his Lordfhip's attention to it; and is well pleafed his Lordfhip has chofen to continue at the head of it. But his Majefty commands me to fignify to you his royal pleafure, that you do immediately acquaint his Lordfhip, that he ftill retains his rank of Lieutenant-colonel in the army.

Inftructions to the Hon. Major-general Leflie, dated Head-Quarters, New-York, October 10, 1780.

SIR,

YOU will be pleafed to proceed with the troops embarked under your command to Chefapeak Bay; and upon your arrival at that place, you will purfue fuch meafures as you fhall judge moft likely to anfwer the purpofe of this expedition; the principal object of which is to make a diverfion in favour of Lieutenant-general Earl Cornwallis, who by the time you arrive there will probably be acting in the back parts of North Carolina. The information you fhall procure

D *

cure on the spot after your arrival at your destined port, will point out to you the properest method of accomplishing this. But from that which I have received here, I should judge it best to proceed up James River as high as possible, in order to seize or destroy any magazines the enemy may have at Petersburg, Richmond, or any of the places adjacent; and finally, to establish a post on Elizabeth River. But this, as well as the direction of every other operation, is submitted to Earl Cornwallis, with whom you are as soon as possible to communicate, and afterwards to follow all such orders and directions you shall from time to time receive from his Lordship.

H. CLINTON.

Extract,— Sir Henry Clinton to Earl Cornwallis, dated New-York, November 6, 1780.

YOUR Lordship can judge of the strength of this part of the army, by that under your own orders; and will agree with me that it is scarcely possible for me to detach a greater force from it, or of our being able to make such efforts in Chesapeak Bay, as are now almost become necessary. However, when I know your Lordship's success in North Carolina, and your determination respecting a post on Elizabeth River, I will then consider what additional force I can spare. If your Lordship determines to withdraw that post, I shall in that case think your present force, including General Leslie's, quite sufficient.

By

By the copy of inſtructions laſt ſent, and thoſe now forwarded to General Leſlie, your Lordſhip will perceive I mean that you ſhould take the command of the whole. If my wiſhes are fulfilled, they are, that you may *eſtabliſh a poſt at Hillſborough, feed it from Croſs Creek, and be able to keep that of Portſmouth.* A few troops will do it, and carry on deſultory expeditions in Cheſapeak, *till more ſolid operations can take place ;* — *of which I fear* there is no proſpect, without we are conſiderably reinforced. The moment I know your Lordſhip's determination to keep a poſt at Portſmouth, I will, as I ſaid before, conſider what additional force I can ſpare. *Once aſſured of our remaining ſuperior at ſea,* I might poſſibly ſend two thouſand more for this winter's operations.

Operations in Cheſapeak are but of two ſorts. Solid operation with a fighting army, to call forth our friends and ſupport them ; or a poſt, ſuch as Portſmouth, carrying on deſultory expeditions ; ſtopping up in a great meaſure the Cheſapeak ; and by commanding James River, prevent the enemy from forming any conſiderable depots upon it, or moving in any force to the ſouthward of it. Such, my Lord, are the advantages I expect from a ſtation at Portſmouth ; and I wiſh it may appear to you in the ſame light.

Second Inſtructions to the Hon. Major-general Leſlie, dated New-York, November 2, 1780.

S I R,

HAVING already put you under the orders of

Lord

Lord Cornwallis, who muſt of courſe be the beſt judge of operations to the ſouthward, it may be needleſs to ſay any thing more. But leſt you ſhould not receive any orders from his Lordſhip, or obtain certain intelligence relative to him; or have reaſon to ſuppoſe you can better aſſiſt his operations by a diverſion made nearer him; I think it neceſſary to give you ſome hints reſpecting Cape Fear River, and how far the acting upon that river may operate. Should Lord Cornwallis have paſſed the Yadkin, and be advanced towards Hillſborough, I think you cannot act any where ſo well as on James River, approaching ſometimes towards the Roanoke, but not paſſing that river without orders from Lord Cornwallis. If you have every reaſon to believe that his Lordſhip meets with oppoſition at his paſſage of the Yadkin, I think a move on Cape Fear River will operate effectually. I have had much converſation with General O'Hara on this ſubject. I have given him every information reſpecting that move; and I truſt after conſulting him you will act in the beſt manner poſſible to fulfill the object of all your inſtructions --- *a diverſion in favour of Lord Cornwallis.* That you may be the better judge of his plan, I ſend you copies of ſuch of his letters, which give any hints towards it.

You will of courſe cautiouſly avoid inrolling any of the militia of Princeſs Anne or elſewhere, without you determine to eſtabliſh a poſt. Thoſe, however, who voluntarily join you muſt be taken care of.

H. CLINTON.

Extract.

Extract. — From Earl Cornwallis to Sir Henry Clinton, dated Camp at Waxhaw, September 22, 1780.

I F nothing material happens to obſtruct my plan of operations, I mean, as ſoon as Lieutenant-colonel Tarleton can be removed, to proceed with the twenty-third, thirty-third, volunteers of Ireland, and Legion, to Charlotte-town, and leave the ſeventy-firſt here until the ſick can be brought on to us. I then mean to make ſome redoubts and eſtabliſh a fixed poſt at that place, and give the command of it to Major Wimys, whoſe regiment is ſo totally demoliſhed by ſickneſs, that it will not be fit for actual ſervice for ſome months. To that place I ſhall bring up all the ſick from Camden, who have any chance of being ſerviceable before Chriſtmas, and truſt to opportunities for their joining the army.

The poſt at Charlotte-town will be a great ſecurity to all this frontier of South-Carolina, which, even if we were poſſeſſed of the greateſt part of North-Carolina, would be liable to be infeſted by parties, who have retired with their effects over the mountains, and mean to take every opportunity of carrying on a predatory war, and it will, I hope, prevent inſurrections in this country, which is very diſaffected. I then think of moving on my principal force to Saliſbury, which will open this country ſufficiently for us to ſee what aſſiſtance we may really expect from our friends in North-Carolina; and will give us a

E   free

free communication with the Highlanders, on whom my greatest dependance is placed.

Extract. — From Earl Cornwallis to Lord George Germain, dated Camp at Waxhaw, September 19, 1780.

MY LORD,

I HAD the honour to inform your Lordship in my letter of the 21st of August, that I had dispatched proper people into North-Carolina to exhort our friends in that province to take arms, to seize military stores, and magazines of the enemy, and to intercept all stragglers of the routed army.

Some parties of our friends, who had embodied themselves near the Pedée, disarmed several of the enemy's stragglers. But the leading persons of the Loyalists were so undecided in their councils, that they lost the critical time of availing themselves of our success; and even suffered General Gates to pass to Hillsborough with a guard of six men only. They continue however to give me the strongest assurances of support, when his Majesty's troops shall have penetrated into the interior parts of the province. The patience and fortitude with which they endure the most cruel torments, and suffer the most violent oppressions that a country ever laboured under, convince me that they are sincere, at least as far as their affection, to the cause of Great-Britain.

PART

P A R T   IV.

CONTAINING

E X T R A C T S

FROM THE

Correfpondence with Earl Cornwallis, &c. from Major
Fergufon's Misfortune to his Lordfhip's fecond Move
into North Carolina.

———————

*Extract. — From Major-general Leflie to Sir Henry
Clinton, dated Portfmouth, Nov. 7, 1780, eight at
Night.*

SIR,

THIS inftant Lieutenant Gratton, of the fixty-
fourth, is arrived exprefs from Charles-town, in his
Majefty's fhip Iris, with a letter from Lord Rawdon,
Lord Cornwallis being a little indifpofed.

I inclofe your Excellency a copy of the contents.
I called on Commodore Gayton, and Brigadier-gene-
ral Howard, for their opinion how we fhould act.
We all agree to go to Cape Fear as foon as poffible.
Very forry it is neceffary ; but my orders from your

E 2   Excel-

Excellency is to co-operate and act with his Lordship to the utmoft of my power.

Copy. — *From Lord Rawdon to Major-general Leflie,
dated Camp, near the Indian Lands, Weft of Cattawba river, South Carolina, Oct. 24, 1780.*

S I R,

LORD Cornwallis not being fufficiently recover-
ed from a fevere fever which lately attacked him to
be able to write to you, his Lordfhip has defired
that I fhould have the honour of communicating
with you upon the fubject of the prefent fervice.
The Commander in Chief has tranfmitted to Lord
Cornwallis a copy of the inftructions under which
you are to act.   At the time when Peterfburgh was
fuggefted as an advifeable point for a diverfion, which
might co-operate with our intended efforts for the
reduction of North Carolina, it was imagined that
the tranquillity of South Carolina was affured ; and
the repeated affurances which were fent to us by the
Loyalifts in North Carolina, gave us reafon to hope,
that their number and their zeal would not only facilitate the reftoration of his Majefty's government
in that province, but might alfo fupply a force for
more extenfive operations.   Events unfortunately
have not anfwered to thefe flattering promifes.   The
appear-

appearance of General Gates's army unveiled to us a fund of difaffection in this province, of which we could have formed no idea ; and even the difperfion of that force did not extinguifh the ferment which the hope of its fupport had raifed. This hour the majority of the inhabitants of that tract between the Pedee and the Santée are in arms againft us ; and when we laft heard from Charles-town, they were in poffeffion of George-town, from which they had diflodged our militia.

It was hoped that the rifing which was expected of our friends in North Carolina might awe that diftrict into quiet ; therefore, after giving them a little chaftifement, by making the feventh regiment take that route in its way to the army, Lord Cornwallis advanced to Charlotteburg.

Major Fergufon, with about eight hundred militia collected from the neighbourhood of Ninety-fix, had previoufly marched into Tryon county to protect our friends, who were fuppofed to be numerous there ; and it was intended, that he fhould crofs the Cattawba river, and endeavour to preferve tranquiility in the rear of the army. A numerous army now appeared on the frontiers, drawn from Nolachucki, and other fettlements beyond the mountains, whofe very names had been unknown to us. A body of thefe, joined by the inhabitants of the ceded lands in Georgia, made a fudden and violent attack upon Augufta. The poft was gallantly defended by Lieutenant-colonel

nel Brown, till he was relieved by the activity of Lieutenant-colonel Cruger : but Major Ferguson, by endeavouring to intercept the enemy in their retreat, unfortunately gave time for fresh bodies of men to pass the mountains, and to unite into a corps far superior to that which he commanded. They came up with him, and after a sharp action entirely defeated him. Ferguson was killed, and all his party either slain or taken.

By the enemy's having secured all the passes on the Cattawba, Lord Cornwallis (who was waiting at Charlotteburg for a convoy of stores) received but confused accounts of the affair for some time : but at length the truth reached him ; and the delay, equally with the precautions the enemy had taken to keep their victory from his knowledge, gave Lord Cornwallis great reason to fear for the safety of Ninety-six. To secure that district was indispensible for the security of the rest of the province ; and Lord Cornwallis saw no means of effecting it, but by passing the Cattawba river with his army ; for it was so weakened by sickness, that it would not bear detachment.

After much fatigue on the march, occasioned by violent rains, we passed the river three days ago. We then received the first intelligence, respecting the different posts in this province, which had reached us for near three weeks ; every express from Camden having been waylaid, and some of them murdered by the inhabitants. — Ninety-six is safe : the corps which defeated Ferguson having, in confequence of our movement, croffed the Cattawba, and joined Smallwood on the Yadkin.

In our prefent pofition we have received the firft intimation of the expedition under your command. From the circumftances which I have detailed, we fear that we are too far afunder to render your co-operation very effectual. No force has prefented it-felf to us, whofe operation could have been thought ferious againft this army : but then we have little hopes of bringing the affair to the iffue of an action. The enemy are moftly mounted militia, not to be overtaken by our infantry, nor to be fafely purfued in this ftrong country by our cavalry. Our fear is, that inftead of meeting us, they would flip by us into this province, were we to proceed far from it, and might again ftimulate the difaffected to ferious infurrection. This apprehenfion you will judge, Sir, muft greatly circumfcribe our efforts. Indeed, Lord Cornwallis cannot hope that he fhall be able to undertake any thing upon fuch a fcale, as either to aid you, or to benefit from you in our prefent fituation. The Com-mander in Chief has fignified to Lord Cornwallis, that his Lordfhip is at liberty to give you any direc-tion for farther co-operation which may appear to him expedient. But his Excellency has complied fo very fully and completely with Lord Cornwallis's requeft, by fending fo powerful a force to make a diverfion in the Chefapeak, that his Lordfhip fears

he

he fhould require too much, were he to draw you into the immediate fervice of this diftri&. His Lord-fhip is likewife delicate on this point, becaufe he does not know how far, by drawing you from the Chefapeak, he might interfere with any other pur-pofes to which the Commander in Chief may have deftined your troops. Under thefe circumftances, Lord Cornwallis thinks himfelf obliged to leave you at liberty to purfue whatever meafures may appear to your judgment beft for his Majefty's fervice, and moft confonant with the wifhes of the Commander in Chief. No time is fpecified to Lord Cornwallis as the limitation of your ftay to the fouthward. Should your knowledge of Sir Henry Clinton's defires prompt you to make a trial upon North Carolina, Cape Fear river appears to us to be the only part where your efforts are at prefent likely to be effectual. A de-fcent there would be the fureft means of joining and arming the friends of government, as well as of co-operating with this army.

This, therefore, would naturally be the point to which Lord Cornwallis would bring you, did he con-ceive himfelf at liberty fo abfolutely to difpofe of you. It muft be remarked, however, that there are two difficulties in this plan; the firft is, that the country from Cape Fear to Crofs-creek (the High-land fettlement) produces fo little, it would be re-quifite in penetrating through it to carry your provi-fions with you; the fecond is, that no veffel larger

than

than a frigate can pafs the bar of Cape Fear harbour. Whatever you decide, Lord Cornwallis defires earneftly to hear from you as foon as poffible.

'Tis uncertain yet what fteps this army (if left to itfelf) muft purfue; but it will be ready at leaft to act vigoroufly in aid to any plan which you may undertake. Lord Cornwallis begs that you will inform the Commander in Chief of our circumftances, and that you will have the goodnefs to mention how highly fenfible his Lordfhip is to the very effectual manner in which his Excellency has endeavoured to eafe the operations of his army. The meafure muft have been attended with the moft favourable confequences, had not accidents, which no forefight could expect, fo greatly altered the complexion of our affairs in this province.

Lord Cornwallis defires me to add how much fatisfaction he fhould feel in having your affiftance upon this fervice, did it promife more favourably for you. But fhould the intentions of the Commander in Chief have left you at liberty to make the attempt at Cape Fear, the fuccefs which would probably attend that effential fervice would be doubly pleafing to Lord Cornwallis, from the opportunity it would moft likely give him of congratulating you in perfon. Allow me to add my hopes that the courfe of the fervice would put it in my power to affure you, perfonally, how much

I have the honour to be, &c.

(Signed)   RAWDON.

F   *Copy*

Copy. — *From Sir Henry Clinton, to Major-General Leslie, dated New-York, November* 12, 1780.

S I R,

I have this morning received your dispatches, and by that dated the 7th instant, I observe your intention of quitting the Chesapeak ; and at the requisition of Earl Cornwallis, made to you in a letter written by Lord Rawdon, that you propose going to Cape Fear River with the force under your command. I entirely approve of your having obeyed Earl Cornwallis's directions and desire on this subject, which I hope will be attended with every favourable advantage.

It is not necessary for me to enter upon the matter of your operations in the Chesapeak, as they will now cease.

I have the honour, &c.

(Signed)   H. CLINTON.

Extract. — *From Major-General Leslie to Sir Henry Clinton, on board the Romulus, dated Hampton Road, November* 19, 1780.

THE people in general seem sorry at our leaving this district, and I believe would have been happy to have remained quiet at home. It is a plentiful
country

country all round our pofts; from my firft hearing of Fergufon's fate, I inwardly fufpected what came to pafs; therefore I never iffued any proclamation of my *own,* nor did I encourage the people to take arms. Many blamed me for it, but now they think I acted right.

I left the works entire, and I ftill hope that you will be able to take up this ground; for it certainly is the key to the wealth of Virginia and Maryland. It is to be lamented we are fo weak in fhips of war, for there is a fleet of fixty fail expected hourly from the Weft Indies, befides the valuable fhips or craft ready to fail from the Chefapeak.

Copy. — From Lord Rawdon to Sir Henry Clinton, camp between Broad River and the Catawba, dated October 29, 1780.

SIR,

LORD Cornwallis having been fo reduced by a fevere fever, as to be ftill unable to write, he has defired that I fhould have the honour of addreffing your Excellency in regard to our prefent fituation. But few days have paft fince Lord Carnwallis received your Excellency's difpatch of the 20th of September. In confequence of it, his Lordfhip directed that I fhould immediately fend a letter to meet Major-General Leflie in the Chefapeak;

giving

giving him the fulleſt information reſpecting our proſpects, and the preſent temper of the country, I have the honour to incloſe a copy of that letter. Something remains to be ſaid in addition to it, of a nature which Earl Cornwallis judged inexpedient to unveil, excepting to your Excellency.

For ſome time after the arrival of his Majeſty's troops at Camden, repeated meſſages were ſent to head quarters, by the friends of government in North Carolina, expreſſing their impatience to riſe and join the King's ſtandard. The impoſſibility of ſubſiſting that additional force at Camden, and the accounts which they themſelves gave of the diſtreſſing ſcarcity, of proviſions in North Carolina, obliged Lord Cornwallis to entreat them to remain quiet, till the new crop might enable us to join them. In the mean time General Gates's army advanced. We were greatly ſurpriſed, and no leſs grieved, that no information whatever of its movements was conveyed to us by perſons ſo deeply intereſted in the event as the North Carolina Loyaliſts. Upon the 16th of Auguſt that army was ſo entirely diſperſed, that it was clear no number of them could for a conſiderable time be collected. Orders were therefore diſpatched to our friends, ſtating that the hour, which they had ſo long preſſed, was arrived; and exhorting them to ſtand forth immediately, and prevent the re-union of the ſcattered enemy. Inſtant ſupport was in that caſe promiſed them. In the fulleſt confidence that this

event

event was to take place, Lord Cornwallis ventured to prefs your Excellency for co-operation in the Chesapeak, hoping that the affiftance of the ... ... Carolinians might eventually furnish a force for yet farther efforts. Not a fingle man, however, attempted to improve the favourable moment, or obeyed that fummons for which they had before been fo impatient. It was hoped that our approach might get the better of their timidity; yet during a long period, whilft we were waiting at Charlotteburgh for our ftores and convalefcents, they did not even furnifh us with the leaft information refpecting the force collecting againft us. In fhort, Sir, we may have a powerful body of friends in North Carolina, — and indeed we have caufe to be convinced, that many of the inhabitants wifh well to his Majefty's arms; but they have not given evidence enough either of their number or their activity, *to juftify the ftake of this province, for the uncertain advantages that might attend immediate junction with them.* There is reafon to believe that fuch muft have been the rifk.

Whilft this army lay at Charlotteburgh, George-Town was taken from the militia by the rebels; and the whole country to the eaft of the Santée, gave fuch proofs of general defection, that even the militia of the High Hills could not be prevailed upon to join a party of troops who were fent to protect our boats upon the river. The defeat of Major Fergufon, had fo difpirited this part of the country, and

indeed

indeed the loyal fubjects were fo wearied by the long continuance of the campaign, that Lieutenant-colonel Cruger, (commanding at Ninety-fix) fent information to Earl Cornwallis, that the whole diftrict had determined to fubmit as foon as the rebels fhould enter it. From thefe circumftances, from the confideration that delay does not extinguifh our hopes in North Carolina; and from the long fatigue of the troops, which made it ferioufly requifite to give fome refrefhment to the army; Earl Cornwallis has refolved to remain for the prefent in a pofition which may fecure the frontiers without feparating his force. In this fituation we fhall be always ready for movement, whenfoever opportunity fhall recommend it, or circumftances require it. But the firft care muft be to put Camden and Ninety-fix into a better ftate of defence, and to furnifh them with ample ftores and falt provifions. Earl Cornwallis forefees all the difficulties of a defenfive war. *Yet his Lordfhip thinks they cannot be weighed against the dangers which muft have attended an obftinate adherence to his former plan.* I am inftructed by Earl Cornwallis to exprefs, in the ftrongeft terms, his Lordfhip's feelings, with regard to the very effectual meafures which your Excellency had taken to forward his operations. His Lordfhip hopes that his fears of abufing your Excellency's goodnefs in that particular, may not have led him to neglect making ufe of a force intended by your

Excellency

Ecellency to be employed by him. But as his Lordfhip knew not how far your Excellency might aim at other objects in the Chefapeak (to which point his Lordfhip's entreaty for co-operation was originally confined) he could not think of affuming the power to order Major-general Leflie to Cape Fear river; though he pointed out the utility of the meafure, in cafe it fhould be conceived within the extent of your Excellency's purpofe.

Lord Cornwallis farther defires me to fay he feels infinitely obliged by the very flattering teftimonies of approbation with which your Excellency has been pleafed to honour his fuccefs on the 16th of Auguft. He has fignified your Excellency's thanks to the officers and men, who received them with grateful acknowledgement.

I have the honour to be, &c.

(Signed) RAWDON.

Extract. — From **Lord Rawdon** *to Sir Henry Clinton, dated Camp between Broad River, and the Catawba, South Carolina, October 31, 1780.*

SIR,

BY Lord Cornwallis's directions, I had the honour of writing to your Excellency on the 29th
Inftant,

Inftant, detailing to your Excellency the circumftances which had obliged Lord Cornwallis to re-
linquifh the attempt of penetrating to Hillfborough ;
and inclofing the copy of a letter which his Lordfhip made me write to Major-general Leflie on that
occafion.

On farther confideration his Lordfhip reflecting on
the difficulties of a defenfive war, and of the hopes
which your Excellency would probably build of our
fuccefs in this quarter, has thought it advifable not
only to recommend more ftrongly to Major-general
Leflie, a plan which may enable us to take an active
part ; but even to make it his requeft in cafe it fhould
not be incompatible with your Excellency's farther
arrangements.

Lord Cornwallis is particularly induced to invite
Major-general Leflie to co-operation in the Cape
Fear river, by the fuppofition that your Excellency
may not want thefe troops during the winter : *and
they may join your Excellency in the fpring, fcarcely
later than, fhould they on the approach of that feafon
fail from any part of Chefapeak Bay.*

Extract. — From Earl Cornwallis to Major-general Leslie, dated Camp at Winnesborough, between Broad River and Wateree, November 12, 1780.

IF you come to Cape Fear, of which at prefent, I have little doubt, by the help of gallies and fmall craft, which will be fent from Charles-town, you will eafily fecure a water conveyance for your ftores up to Crofs Creek. I will on hearing of your arrival in Cape Fear river, inftantly march with every thing that can be fafely fpared from this Province, which I am forry to fay is moft exceedingly difaffected, to join you at Crofs Creek. We will then give our friends in North Carolina, a fair trial. If they behave like men it may be of the greateft advantage to the affairs of Britain. If they are as ————— as our friends to the fouthward, we muft leave them to their fate; *and fecure what we have got.*

————————————

Extract. — From Lieutenant-colonel Balfour, without date, to Major-general Leslie.

MY DEAR GENERAL;

I WROTE you a few days ago by the Exprefs floop, and have only to repeat, that the *fafety* of this province *now* is concerned in your getting as faft

G

as poffible near us. ———— Gates is advancing as we are told, to this province, and already near it.

———————————

Copy. — *From Sir Henry Clinton, K. B. to Earl Cornwallis, dated New York, December* 13, 1780.

MY LORD,

I A M honoured with your Lordfhip's letters of the 3d and 22d of September, by the Thames, which arrived here the 12th ultimo. And on the 5th inftant I received by the Beaumont, thofe from Lord Rawdon, and Colonel Balfour, to General Leflie. Inclofed I fend your Lordfhip a return of the force that embarked with him.

It was all I could fpare; and I thought it fully adequate to the fervices required. My firft inftructions to General Leflie put that corps entirely fubject to your Lordfhip's orders.

I did not, I confefs, however fuppofe it would move to Cape Fear ; but having afterwards too good reafon to dread Fergufon's fate, I in a fecond inftruction recommended that meafure, as the only falutary one under the circumftances I apprehended Fergufon's defeat would place your Lordfhip. By a letter of Colonel Balfour's to General Leflie (without date) are thefe Expreffions " I have only to repeat that the *fafety* of this province *now* is concerned in your

getting

getting as fast as possible near us." I should be sorry to understand by this that the province is really in danger. Wishing however to give your Lordship's operations in North Carolina, every assistance in my power, though I can ill spare it, I have sent another expedition into the Chesapeak, under the orders of Brigadier-general Arnold, Lieutenant-colonels Dundas, and Simcoe. The force by land is not equal to that which sailed with General Leslie ; but I am not without hopes it will operate most essentially in favour of your Lordship ; either by striking at Gates's depot at Petersburg, which I have still reason to think is considerable ; or finally by taking post at Portsmouth, which I have ever considered as very important, for reasons most obvious. If we take post there, fortify, and assemble the inhabitants ; it ought not afterwards to be quitted ; and therefore I cannot suppose your Lordship will wish to alter the disposition of this corps, without absolute necessity.

On the contrary I flatter myself, that should your success be such as your Lordship will, I hope, *now* have reason to expect, that you will reinforce that corps, and enable it to act offensively. When that is your intention, I am to request that the following corps may in their turn be considered for that service, *viz.* The troop of seventeenth dragoons, the yagers, the detachment of the seventeenth foot, and the provincial light infantry, &c. I need not tell your Lordship that these detachments have left

G 2

n*

me very bare indeed of troops ; nor that Wafhington ftill continues very ftrong (at leaft 12000 men) that he has not detatched a fingle man as yet to the fouth- ward, except Lee's cavalry (about two hundred and fifty). I need not tell you alfo that there are fix thou- fand French already at Rhode Ifland — but I muft acquaint your Lordfhip that fix complete regiments more are expected, under convoy of a number of capital fhips. But whatever may have been the in- tention of the French in fending a reinforcement to this country, I think the feafon is now too far ad- vanced to expect the laft ; and was I not clearly of that opinion I fhould fcarcely dare detatch as I do. As I have always faid, I think your Lordfhip's movement to the fouthward moft important, and as I ever have done, fo I will now give them all the affiftance I can. It remains to be proved whether we have friends in North Carolina — I am fure we had three years ago — That experiment now will *be fairly tried*; if it fucceeds, and we hold the entrance of the Chefapeak — I think the rebels will fcarcely rifk another attempt upon thofe provinces.

Copy.

Copy. — *From Earl Cornwallis to Sir Henry Clinton, dated Camp at Wynnefborough, December 3, 1780.*

S I R,

I AM honoured with your letters of the 5th and 6th of laft month. Lord Rawdon, during my illnefs, informed your Excellency, in his letters of the 28th and 31ft of October, of the various caufes which prevented my penetrating into North Carolina. I fhall not trouble you with a recapitulation, except a few words about poor Major Fergufon. I had the honour to inform your Excellency that Major Fergufon had taken infinite pains with fome of the militia of Ninety-fix. He obtained my permiffion to make an incurfion into Tryon county, while the ficknefs of my army prevented my moving. As he had only militia and the fmall remains of his own corps, without baggage or artillery, and as he promifed to come back if he heard of any fuperior force, I thought he could do no harm, and might help to keep alive the fpirit of our friends in North Carolina, which might be damped by the flownefs of our motions. The event proved unfortunate, without any fault of Major Fergufon's. A numerous and unexpected enemy came from the mountains. As they had good horfes,

their

their movements were rapid. Major Ferguson was tempted to stay near the mountains longer than he intended, in hopes of cutting off Colonel Clarke on his return from Georgia. He was not aware that the enemy was so near him; and, in endeavouring to execute my orders of passing the Catawba, and joining me at Charlotte-town, he was attacked by a very superior force, and totally defeated on King's-mountain.

Wynnesborough, my present position, is an healthy spot, well situated to protect the greatest part of the Northern frontier, and to assist Camden and Ninety-six. The militia of the latter, on which alone we could place the smallest dependence, was so totally dispirited by the defeat of Ferguson, that of the whole district we could with difficulty assemble one hundred; and even those, I am convinced, would not have made the smallest resistance if they had been attacked. I determined to remain at this place until an answer arrived from General Leslie, on which my plan for the winter was to depend; and to use every possible means of putting the province into a state of defence, which I found to be absolutely necessary, whether my campaign was offensive or defensive. Bad as the state of our affairs was on the Northern frontier, the Eastern part was much worse. Colonel Tynes, who commanded the militia of the high hills of Santee, and who was posted on Black-river, was surprized and taken, and his men lost all their arms. Colonel Marion had so wrought on the minds of the people, partly by the terror of his threats and cruelty of his punishments; and partly by the promise of plunder, that there was scarcely an inhabitant between the Santée and Pedée, that was not in arms against us. Some parties had even crossed the Santée, and carried terror to the gates of Charles-town. My first object was to reinstate matters in that quarter, without which Camden could receive no supplies. I therefore sent Tarleton, who pursued Marion for several days, obliged his corps to take to the swamps, and by convincing the inhabitants that there was a power superior to Marion, who could likewise reward and punish, so far checked the insurrection, that the greatest part of them have not dared to appear in arms against us since his expedition. ——

—— As it will be necessary to drive back the enemies army, and at the same time to maintain a superiority on both our flanks; and as I thought the co-operation of General Leslie, even at the distance of Cape-Fear river, would be attended with many difficulties, I have sent cruizers off the Frying-pan to bring him into Charles-town, and I hourly expect his arrival.

After every thing that has happened, I will not presume to make your Excellency any san-

guine

guine promifes.   *The force you have fent me is greater than I expected; and full as much as I think you could poffibly fpare,* unlefs the enemy detached in force to the Southward.   The utmoft exertion of my abilities fhall be ufed to employ them to the beft advantage.

Whenever our operations commence, your Ex-cellency may depend on hearing from me as fre-quently as poffible; and it is from events alone that any future plan can be propofed.

Extract. ----- *From Earl Cornwallis to Sir Henry Clinton, dated Wynnefborough, Dec. 22, 1780.*

S I R,

I HAVE the honour to inform your Excellency, that Major-general Leflie arrived with his whole fleet at Charles-town on the 14th of this month, with no other lofs. than the dragoon horfes, and a great part of thofe for the Quarter-mafter-general. The fpecies of troops which compofe the rein-forcement are, exclufive of the Guards and regi-ment of Bofe, exceedingly bad.*   I do not mean,

by

---

* When his Lordfhip made this remark, he had not feen the troops. He muft have, therefore, formed his opinion from the report of others. But in juftice to the corps who are fpoken fo flightingly of, it is ne-ceffary

by reprefenting this to your Excellency, to infinu-
ate, that you have not fent every affiftance to me
which you could with prudence and fafety fpare
from New-York. From the account which your
Excellency does me the honour to fend me, of
the fituation and ftrength of General Wafhington's
army, and the French force at Rhode-Ifland, I am
convinced that you have done fo. But I think it
but juftice to the troops ferving in this diftrict
to ftate the fact, left the fervices performed by
the Southern army fhould appear inadequate to
what might be expected from the numbers of
which it may appear to confift. The fleet from
New-York, with the recruits, arrived a few days
before General Leflie. ————

ceffary to obferve, that they have all behaved in fuch
a manner as to merit the applaufes of the officers commanding them, and one of them (Fannings) has obtained a Britifh eftablifhment.

PART V.

EXTRACTS

FROM THE

Correfpondence; between his Lordfhip's fecond Move into North Carolina, and his Arrival at Wilmington.

Extract. — From Earl Cornwallis to Sir Henry Clinton, dated Wynnefborough, Jan. 6, 1781.

SIR,

I AM juft honoured with your letter of the 13th ult. I have written feveral letters in the courfe of laft month, to give your Excellency an account of the ftate of the provinces of South Carolina and Georgia, and of the military tranfactions. I fear they are all ftill at Charles-town, as no opportunity has offered of tranfmitting them to New-York. The prefent addition to the naval

force

force in this quarter, will, I hope, enable me; or, if I am too diſtant, Lieutenant-colonel Balfour, to tranſmit reports more frequently.

The difficulties I have had to ſtruggle with, have not been occaſioned by the oppoſite army. They always keep at a conſiderable diſtance, and diſappear on our approach.

But the conſtant incurſions of Refugees, North Carolinians, and Back-Mountain-men, and the perpetual riſings in the different parts of this province; the invariable ſucceſſes of all theſe parties againſt our militia, keep the whole country in continual alarm, and renders the aſſiſtance of regular troops every where neceſſary. Your Excellency will judge of this by the diſpoſition of the troops, which I have the honour to encloſe to you.

I ſhall begin my march to-morrow, (having been delayed a few days by a diverſion made by the enemy towards Ninety-ſix) and propoſe keeping on the Weſt of Catawba for a conſiderable diſtance. I ſhall then proceed to paſs that river, and the Yadkin. Events alone can decide the future ſteps. I ſhall take every opportunity of communicating with Brigadier-general Arnold.

Extract.

Extract. — *From Major-general Leslie to Sir Henry Clinton, dated Camden, Jan.* 8, 1781.

SIR,

I ARRIVED here some days ago, with the Guards, the regiment of Bose, and Yagers; I went to Wynnesborough to see Earl Cornwallis. He moves to-day, and I march to-morrow with the above troops and North-Carolina regiment. I meet his Lordship about seventy miles from hence.

The troops are exceeding healthy, and the weather has been very favourable.

Copy. — *From Sir Henry Clinton to Earl Cornwallis, dated New-York, March* 2, 5, *and* 8, 1781.

[Sent by Captain Amherst, in the Jupiter Merchant Ship.]

March 2d.

MY LORD,

YOUR Lordship may probably hear, that the army and navy in the Chesapeak are blocked up by a superior French naval force to that under Captain Symonds. The first account I had of it

I   was

was from General Arnold, dated February 14, and I fent it immediately to the Admiral at Gardiner's-bay. A day or two afterwards I had it confirmed, that they were part of the fleet from Rhode-ifland, which I have heard fince failed from thence on the 9th ult. Notwithftanding which I greatly fear he has not fent a naval force to relieve them. Wafhington has detached fome New-England troops under La Fayette and Howe that way.

March 5th.

IF fo much time is given, I cannot anfwer for confequences. Portfmouth is fafe at this feafon againft any attack from the Suffolk fide, but not fo from a landing in any of the bays to the Southward of Elizabeth-river.

I have much to lament that the Admiral did not think it advifable to fend there at firft, as Brigadier-general Arnold's move in favour of your Lordfhip's operations will have been ftopped. — And if the Admiral delays it too long, I fhall dread ftill more fatal confequences.

I have troops already embarked in a great proportion to that of the enemy, but to fend them under two frigates only, before the Chefapeak is our own, is to facrifice the troops and their convoy.

I enclofe

I enclose your Lordship all the news I have been able to collect. —— —— has, I think, quitted Congress, and put them at defiance. — Your Lordship will see his plan by the newspaper of the 28th of February, said to be genuine. Discontent runs high in Connecticut. In short, my Lord, there seems little wanting to give a mortal stab to rebellion but a proper reinforcement and a superiority at sea for the next campaign; without which, any enterprize depending on water movements must certainly run great risk. Should the troops already embarked for the Chesapeak proceed, and, when there, be able to undertake any operation in addition to what Brigadier-general Arnold proposes, I am confident it will be done. Major-general Phillips will command this expedition.

Till Colonel Bruce arrives, I am uncertain what reinforcements are intended for this army. The minister has, however, assured me, that every possible exertion will be made.

I shall tremble for our post at Portsmouth, should the enemy's reinforcement arrive in that neighbourhood before the force, which I *now* flatter myself the Admiral will order a sufficient convoy for, arrives.

March

March 8th.

I HAVE received a letter from General Arnold, dated the 25th ult. wherein he tells me, that the French left him on the 19th.

And in another letter, of the 27th, he says, he has not the least doubt of defending his post against the force of the country and two thousand French troops, until a reinforcement can arrive from New-York. And that he proposed to send five hundred men, under Colonel Dundas, up James-river, to make a diversion in favour of your Lordship.

The Admiral informs me of the return of the French ships to Rhode-island, and of their having taken the Romulus, and carried her into that place. But as the Admiral, in his letter of the 4th, seems to think, that the whole, or at least a great part of the French fleet sailed for the Chesapeak on the 27th ult, and that he was at that time ready to sail, I flatter myself he is either gone there, or has sent a sufficient force to clear the Chesapeak. The troops under General Phillips have been embarked for some time, and are now at the Hook waiting for the Admiral, or a message from him. General Phillips commands, and I am sure you know his inclinations are to

co-operate

co-operate with your Lordfhip; and you will therefore be pleafed to take him under your orders, until you hear farther from me.

I have the honour, &c.

(Signed) H. CLINTON.

Extract. — From Brigadier-general Arnold to Sir Henry Clinton, K. B. dated Portfmouth, January 23, 1781.

T H E line of works begun, which are neceffary for the defence of this place, your Excellency will ob-ferve (by the plan inclofed) are very extenfive, and from the fituation of it, cannot be contracted. The engineer's opinion of them, and the number of men neceffary for their defence, againft a fuperior force, I do myfelf the honour to inclofe. Lieutenant-colonels Dundas and Simcoe, are clearly of opinion with me, that three thoufand men are neceffary for their de-fence. We have all been greatly deceived in the ex-tent and nature of the ground. There are many places in the river much eafier defended with half the number of men. From the fketch of the place your Excellency will judge whether our opinion is well founded or not.

This province and North Carolina, are collecting the militia, undoubtedly with a view to pay us a vifit. Their numbers, from the beft information I can ob-tain, are four thoufand or five thoufand. At prefent I can hardly imagine they will attack this poft, though the works are of no manner of fervice to us ; and all our force cannot complete them in three months : I therefore think it my duty to requeft a reinforcement of at leaft two thoufand men, which would render the poft permanent and fecure againft

I   any

any force the country could bring, as detachments could always be made (leaving the garrifon fecure) to difperfe the militia, whenever it was found they were collecting; and the advantages of tranfportation, which we may derive from light boats (of which I propofe to build fifty) would enable us to move with double the celerity, that the militia could do with every exertion.

The country people have not come in, in numbers, as I expected; the neceffity of General Leflie's removing from this place, after their being affured of his intention to remain here, has impreffed them with the idea that we fhall do the fame; which is not eafily effaced, as they have many of them fuffered feverely fince his departure. I have not with certainty been informed where he is at prefent — Reports, which are contradictory, fay at Cape Fear; others that he is at Charles-town; and fome fay at neither. I know not what opinion to form; neither have I heard from Lord Cornwallis, but by reports, which fay he is at or near Camden — No opportunity has yet prefented of writing to either of thefe gentlemen — but I am of opinion our diverfion at Richmond will operate much in his favour, as I am informed the militia and light-horfe, fent to reinforce the rebel army, under Greene, have been ordered to return.

Extract.

Extract. — *From Sir Henry Clinton, K. B. to General Earl Cornwallis, dated New York, February 5, 1781.*

MY LORD,

I HAVE the honour to inclofe to your Lord-fhip the copy of a letter I have lately received from Brigadier-general Arnold, by which you will perceive that with fcarcely one thoufand men (for feveral of his tranfports, that had been feparated on the voyage, had not then rejoined him) he penetrated to Richmond, the capital of Virginia, and has rendered important fervice, by deftroying a valuable foundry, a confiderable quantity of public ftores, cannon, &c. &c. Indeed the whole of his operations upon the occafion appear to have been conducted in a manner which ftrongly marks his character of a very active and good officer — and I fincerely hope, that this important ftroke will effentially aid your Lordfhip's operations.

I 2

Extract.

Extract. — *From Sir H. Clinton, K. B. to Lieutenant-colonel Balfour, sent by Captain Amherst, in the Jupiter merchant ship, dated New York, March 9, 1781.*

SIR,

I WAS favoured with your letters, dated the 25th and 31ft January, and 2d and 5th February, by the Halifax floop of war, on the 16th ultimo.

Captain Amherst of the fixtieth regiment, who is fo obliging to charge himfelf with my difpatches for Lord Cornwallis, will deliver them to your care.

———

Extract. — *From Brigadier-general Arnold to Sir H. Clinton, K. B. dated Portfmouth, February 13, 1781.*

NO time has been loft in repairing the old, and erecting new works here, in which the negroes have been very ferviceable, but none are yet complete. Repairing barracks, foraging, and patrolling with large parties, have engroffed the time of a great part of the troops. One hundred men are pofted at the great bridge.

Lieutenant-colonel Simcoe, with near four hundred men, are in Princefs Anne county; fcouring the county of feveral parties, and arranging matters with the country people.

The

The enemy are at Suffolk, with two thousand five hundred, or three thousand men; they threaten an attack upon us, but I cannot suppose them capable of so much temerity. We are prepared for them at all points, and I believe nothing will induce them to attack us, but the hope of succeeding in a surprise, and despair of keeping their tattered force together, through want of provisions, and the necessity of their ploughing their lands, to prevent a famine the ensuing year.

Extract. — *From Brigadier general Arnold to Sir H. Clinton, K. B. dated Portsmouth, February* 25, 1781.

A F T E R my dispatches were closed (which were intended to go by the General Monk) three French ships, one a sixty-four, the other two frigates, arrived from Rhode Island, and anchored in Lynhaven Bay. On the 14th instant they arrived in Hampton road, and remained there until the 19th, when they left the Capes, and are said to be now cruizing to the southward of them.

Before the arrival of the French ships, the enemy's force did not exceed two thousand five hundred men, at Suffolk and in the vicinity, which was greatly

2   augmented

augmented soon after their arrival. On the 18th they came down in force, near our lines, and surprised a piquet of six men ; but soon retired. Lieutenant-colonel Simcoe with four hundred men being in Princess Anne county, I did not think it prudent to leave our works to attack them.

I have very good intelligence that the rebels at Suffolk have been informed by express from General Greene, that on the 16th or 18th instant, my Lord Cornwallis crossed the Dan river, sixty miles above Halifax, and one hundred and twelve from Petersburgh, with one thousand cavalry and four thousand infantry, and was on the march for Petersburgh. Generals Greene and Morgan, with three thousand or four thousand men, chiefly militia, were retiring before him ; in consequence of which a considerable part of their troops, have been detached to join General Greene. I have not been able to ascertain the number of troops remaining at Suffolk and in the vicinity ; I expect to do it in a day or two, in which time every possible effort shall be made to complete our works in such a manner, that a considerable detachment may be made to proceed up the James river, with some ships to co-operate with Lord Cornwallis ; and if he should have reached the river, to furnish him with such supplies of provisions, &c. as we can spare, and his troops be most in need of.

Extract.

Extract. — *From Sir Henry Clinton, K. B. to Brigadier-general Arnold, dated New York, February
18, 1781.*

A P P E A R A N C E S at Rhode Ifland give me
reafon to fuppofe that the fhips feen laft Wednef-
day were the avant garde from that place.
Should they pay you a vifit from Rhode Ifland, you
may reft affured every attention will be paid to ur
fituation, and that our movements will be regu ated
by theirs.

I am afraid Tarleton's affair is too true ; but I
have reafon notwithftanding to believe Lord Cornwallis is far advanced in Carolina.

———————————

Extract. — *From Brigadier-general Arnold to Sir H.
Clinton, K. B. dated Portfmouth, February 27, 1781.*

I H A V E not the leaft doubt that every poffible
attention will be paid to our fituation. We are under no apprehenfions at prefent from the force of the
country ; and if the French fhould detach from Rhode
Ifland to this place, I have not the leaft doubt of
defending it againft the force of the country and two
thoufand French troops, until a reinforcement can
arrive from New York.

To-

To-morrow I intend embarking fome ftores, and the next day about five hundred troops under the orders of Lieutenant-colonel Dundas, to proceed up the James river, to make a diverfion in favour of my Lord Cornwallis.

———————

Copy. — Sir Henry Clinton, K. B. to Brigadier-general Arnold, dated New York, March 1, 1781.

S I R,

I S U P P O S E of courfe that the admiral, who knew your fituation on the 21 ft, and heard at the fame time, that the fixty-four and two frigates were from Rhode Ifland, has detached to your relief; — left he fhould not, I have repeatedly preffed him to do it fince.

The French fleet has not yet failed from Rhode Ifland; if it does, encumbered with troops, the admiral will of courfe follow without incumbrance; and, when he has fixed them, it will be time enough to fend troops. In cafe a fleet fhould appear under French colours, do not be alarmed, as I fhall advife the admiral to fend in that manner, to deceive the enemy.

There is information of from twelve to fourteen hundred troops being at Brunfwick the 27th of February, on their way to the fouthward. Thefe it is our bufinefs to watch.

The

- The troops which are all ready embarked, are detained till I receive certain advice that the French ships are removed from the Chesapeak, there being nothing here but frigates to convoy them.

I have received a letter this day from the admiral, dated the 4th: he has given me no possitive information of the movements of the French; he will send a ship to observe their situation in Rhode Island, and will proceed accordingly. Should he call here, the troops will in all probability sail with him; if he does not, I shall send them as soon as I know the way to the Chesapeak is clear.

Extract.—*From Instructions to Major-general Phillips, dated New York, March 10, 1781.*

SIR,

YOU will be pleased to proceed with the troops embarked under your command, to Chesapeak Bay; and there form a junction as soon as possible with brigadier-general Arnold, whom, and the corps with him, you will take under your orders.

When you shall have formed your junction with Brigadier general Arnold, if you find that General acting under the orders of Earl Cornwallis, you will of course endeavour to fulfil those orders. If this

K   should

should not be the case; after receiving every information respecting his probable situation, you will
make such movements with the corps (*then* under
your orders), as can be made confistent with the security of the post on Elizabeth river, or you shall
think will most effectually assist his Lordship's operations; by destroying or taking any magazines, the
enemy may have on James river, or at Petersburg, on
the Appamatox.

The object of co-operation with Lord Cornwallis,
being fulfilled, you are at liberty to carry on such
desultory expeditions for the purpose of destroying the
enemy's public stores and magazines in any part of
the Chesapeak as you shall judge proper.

If the admiral's disapproving of Portsmouth, and
requiring a fortified station for large ships in the Chesapeak, should propose *York Town,* or *Old Point
Comfort,* if possession of either can be acquired and
maintained *without great risk, or loss,* you are at liberty to take possession thereof. *But if the objections
are such as you think forcible, you must, after stating
those objections, decline it, till solid operation take place
in the Chesapeak.*

Concerning your return to this place, you will re
ceive either my orders, or Lord Cornwallis's, as circumstances may make necessary.

It is probable that when the objects of this expedition are fulfilled, and you have strengthened the present works, and added such others as you shall think
necessary,

neceffary, you *may return to this place.* In which cafe you muft bring with you, Brigadier-general Arnold, the light infantry, Colonel Robinfon's corps, or the feventy-fixth; and if it fhould be poffible, the Queen's rangers. The moment you have communicated with Lord Cornwallis, and heard from his Lordfhip, you are to confider yourfelf as under his Lordfhip's orders, until he, or you fhall hear further from me.

(Signed) H. CLINTON.

Extract. — From Brigadier-general Arnold to Sir Henry Clinton, dated Portfmouth, March 8, 1781.

ON the 6th I received information that Lord Cornwallis had not penetrated further than the Dan or Roanoke river, and that, in confequence of the mif-information (fent to the rebel army, by exprefs, as mentioned in my laft) being contradicted, their detachment had returned to their army at Suffolk, as well as Mr. Gregory, to the north-weft bridge — Their force at the former place three thoufand, at the latter five hundred. On this change of affairs the troops under the orders of Lieutenant-colonel Dundas, who were defigned up the James river, were countermanded.

K 2   The

The enemy within two days have moved with their force, said to be upwards of three thousand men to Pricket mills, twelve miles from this place, and threaten an attack upon us. I have every rerfon to believe they have collected their force to co-operate with the French ships and troops, which they hourly expect from Rhode island.

Extract. — *From Admiral Arbuthnot to General Arnold, dated Chefapeak, March 19, 1781.*

THE French fleet failed from Rhode-island on or about the 8th inftant, intending a co-operation with Mr. Washington, to attack you. I followed them on the 10th, and came up with them on the 16th: an action enfued of about an hour and an half, when they fled off with their whole fquadron.

I shall put to fea again immediately with the fquadron, and endeavour to bring them to a fecond action. Should I be unable to do fo, I shall return with the fquadron to New York, which muft be expofed in my abfence, and I muft withdraw the ships that are now with you.

Extract.

Extract. — *From Major-general Phillips to Sir Henry Clinton, dated Chesapeak, on board the Royal Oak, in Lynhaven Bay, March 26, 1781.*

THE fleet containing the troops under my orders, arrived off the Chesapeak yesterday, when Captain Hudson gave the Orpheus liberty to make sail and carry me into this bay, where we knew by intelligence from frigates we met at sea, that Admiral Arbuthnot was with his fleet.

Our fleet sailed from the Hook on Tuesday the 20th instant, and with variable winds, and good weather, is arrived; and now beating up to the rendezvous at Hampton, with hopes, not a certainty, of getting there this evening.

With respect to intelligence, it is not in my power to give you any at a certainty. I hear that at York the rebels have been and are fortifying, and that there are heavy cannon there.

Extract. — *From Sir Henry Clinton to Major-general Phillips, dated New York, March 24, 1781.*

I BELIEVE that Lord Cornwallis has finished his campaign, and if report says true, very handsomely, by taking all Greene's cannon, and recovering the

the greatest part of his own men who had been made
prisoners by Mr. Greene. If that should be the case,
and Lord Cornwallis should not want any co-operation to assist him, and you see no prospect of striking
an important stroke elsewhere, I shall probably request you and General Arnold to return to me with
such troops as I have already named in my instructions. But all this will depend on the information
I shall receive from you, and your opinion, respecting
the post of Portsmouth, and such others as you propose to establish on James river, with their importance, considered, either as assisting Lord Cornwallis's operations, or connected with those of the
navy.

You will probably hear from Lord Cornwallis
before you determine on any attempt at a distance
from him. I wish much to know what force he
can spare from the troops under his Lordship's immediate orders; for till I do, it is impossible to fix
any plan. Three complete regiments will, I hope,
arrive at Charles-town, in the course of a few days, if
Captain Elphinston should think it too early in the
season to come directly here; and three more are
hourly expected from the West-Indies; both which
divisions will of course join me.

The French certainly expect an early reinforcement. If it comes from Europe, we must, I think,
hear from thence long before it arrives; if from the
Havannah, copper-bottomed sloops or frigates, which
the

the admiral will doubtlefs have on the look-out, will announce their arrival, and give you time to determine, what in that cafe, is beft to be done.

And here, I take the liberty of hinting to you, that (from the appearance on the map when you have once obtained a naval force in Curratuck and Albemarle founds, by holding the bridges of Pequimans and Pafquotank rivers, you fecure a fhort paffage acrofs the Albemarle found, and communication with Lord Cornwallis; or, by deftroying the bridges on thofe rivers, you prevent the enemy's approach by the bridge at Northweft-landing.

Extract. — *Major General Phillips to Sir Henry Clinton, K. B. dated Portfmouth, April* 3, 1781.

I have from the moment of my landing here, purfued the firft object of your Excellency's inftructions: " The fecurity of the poft upon Elizabeth " river, near the mouth of James river."

And your Excellency may be affured, I fhall ufe every means to attain this very material purpofe, fo neceffary, and which alone can enable me, with four thoufand militia in our front and near us, to purfue the fecond part of your inftructions: " A move in force

force upon the enemy's communications between Virginia and North Carolina, at Peterſburgh, in aſſiſtance to Lord Cornwallis." And I ſhall do this the moment it may be poſſible, conſiſtent with the ſecurity of the poſt on Elizabeth river.

It is unlucky for us, that we know ſo little of Lord Cornwallis, in favour of whom, and his operations we are directed by your Excellency to exert our utmoſt attention. I ſhall do all in my power to aſſiſt and co-operate with his Lordſhip, and ſhall from inclination, as well as in obedience to your Excellency's inſtructions, do all I can to effect this moſt deſirable end.

I apprehend from various rebel accounts that Lord Cornwallis, although he kept the field, has ſuffered very much after the action of the 15th ultimo, and to be fortifying to the weſt of the *Haw* river, near Guildford, which ſeems a good poſition, having that river in front of the communication quite down to Croſs-Creek and Cape Fear.

Should his Lordſhip want ſupport, he muſt in courſe draw it from Charles-town to Cape Fear river, by directing Lord Rawdon to abandon the frontier, and keep only a garriſon in Charles-town.

I embrace your idea, Sir, that ſhould La Fayette remain at Annapolis, which muſt proceed from the enemy's fear of being attacked in Maryland, it will be poſſible to carry him Annapolis and Baltimore; and if you will ſend me the Britiſh grenadiers and

forty-

forty-fecond regiment, I will, with almoft certain hopes of fuccefs, go upon the attempt; and will make an expedition in Virginia at the fame inftant, as fhall effectually prevent any fupport from thence to Maryland.

. I come now to the particulars of this poft, and as it is not poffible in fo fhort a time, to go through the proper form of a regular report of the commanding engineer, who came with me, I will, until that can be done, very freely offer my opinion that it has not been, I fhould imagine, properly explained to your Excellency, by Generals Matthews and Leflie. The object of the poft, from its fituation, refpecting James river and the Chefapeak, with its connection with the waters to and in Albemarle found, and the confequent connections it may have with any army in the Carolinas, are fubjects I do not think myfelf at liberty to touch upon. I mean to confine myfelf merely to the locality of the poft itfelf; and under that defcription, I declare, I think the prefent fituation not calculated for a poft of force, or for one for a fmall number of troops. In the firft idea, I think three points fhould be taken, as at *Mill Point* and *Norfolk* pofitively; the third muft depend on more examination of the Elizabeth river, than I have yet been able to give. Thefe points taken would mutually affift the navy ftationed here, which might lay within, and be protected; and one point forced, a retreat is left by the other two: and your Excel-

L.   lency

lency will immediately obferve, that it muft require a large force indeed, to attack the three points at once.

Should it be required by your Excellency merely to keep a poft here, without intending more than a ftation, I think Mill Point, where the old fort ftood, well calculated for fuch a purpofe; and it would require not more than a ftrong battalion equal to fix hundred effective rank and file to be the garrifon.

In both inftances the Chefapeak muft be fecure, for even allowing every exertion of defence againft a fleet, it would be difficult to preferve the river under the firft idea of an extenfive plan. Under the latter, I confider it fcarcely to be done. Old Point Comfort fhall be explored, as it feems a point which a fmall force might defend, and the fhipping have fcope to act in, and by trying various methods of winds and tides, would be able poffibly to efcape from even a fuperior naval force; whereas, once blocked up in Elizabeth river, the fhips muft at laft fall with the poft.

I come now to the Norfolk and Princefs Ann counties, where we cannot much depend for affiftance. They are timorous, cautious, at beft, but half friends, and perhaps fome, if not many, concealed enemies. Suppofing them perfectly ours, we fhould not be able to arm more than five or fix hundred men, who would become a charge to us while we remained, and being left, would be undone. At prefent, they act a fort of faving game, but are of no ufe to us. Upon the whole, Sir, it may be perceived that I lean in favour of a fmall poft, where the army can affift the navy, and the latter have a chance of efcaping, fuppofing a fuperior force to arrive in the bay; and where the poft can be maintained with five or fix hundred men, for fome time, even perhaps till fome reinforcement *naval* and land might be fent to raife a fiege.

Copy. — *Sir Henry Clinton, K. B. to Major-general Phillips, dated New-York, April 5,* 1781.

DEAR SIR,

I NEED not fay how important fuccefs in the Highlands would be. I beg you will without lofs of time, confult General Arnold upon the fubject. I beg I may have his project, and your opinion, as well as his, refpecting it, as foon as poffible. When I have confidered it, and if I determine to undertake it, I will fend for him; and if operation fhould be at a ftand in the Chefapeak at the time, I will requeft you alfo to be of the party; the proportion of artillery I defired you to make, will of courfe be ready.

P. S. If General Arnold does not think it expedient at *this time* to attempt it, which however, I should be sorry for, perhaps a combined move between us against Philadelphia, may take place. You, by landing at the head of Elk; I, at Newcastle, or Chester;—if the first, General Arnold must let me have his plan as soon as possible, and be ready to follow it himself, or may bring it, if you can spare him.

Extract. — *Sir Henry Clinton, K. B. to Major-general Phillips, dated New-York, April* 13, 1781.

In addition to what I have said in those letters (April 5) I scarce need mention, that I am persuaded you will not delay to make such movements in favour of Lord Cornwallis as you judge best, with the force you have left after garrisoning the different works at Portsmouth; which after reading the report of your engineer, I flatter myself will be perfectly secure with six or eight hundred men. In that case you will be at liberty to act with the remainder, being as good troops as any in this country, in such operations as you shall judge most conducive to assist those of his Lordship.

Extract

Extract.—Major-general Phillips to Sir Henry Clinton, dated Portsmouth, in Virginia, April 15, 1781.

I AM free to declare Portsmouth to be a bad post, its locality not calculated for defence, the collateral points neceffary to be taken up fo many, that altogether it would require fo great a number of troops as no general officer I imagine would venture to propofe to the Commander-in-chief to leave here for mere defence —— A fpot might be found, I apprehend, for a poft for five hundred men, fhould it be neceffary to have one in Elizabeth River.

Extract. — Major-general Phillips to Sir Henry Clinton, dated Hampton Road, on board the Maria, April 19, 1781.

THE face of affairs feems changed, and the Carolinas, like all America, are loft in rebellion. My letters of the 15th, 16th, and yefterday, will go now in the Amphitrite, for I ftopped the exprefs boat laft night. — I have nothing farther to add, than that I conceive Lord Cornwallis will not have it in his power to bring with him many troops, it will depend on your Excellency from his Lordfhip's

letters,

letters, and from thofe of Brigdier-general Arnold and me, whether you fhall think it proper to have an operation in force in Chefapeak — if yes, the troops here are too few — if no, too many.

I hope to hear from your Excellency directly, and perhaps it may not be fo well to truft fuch a ferious difpatch, as your next, Sir, will probably be, to an unarmed veffel, but that a frigate will be fent.

The operations I had propofed againft Williamf-burg, fhall take place to-morrow morning, but I think it my duty to call a council of war, circum-ftanced as Lord Cornwallis is, to judge whether an attempt on Peterfburg may now be proper.

Extract. — Lieutenant-colonel Balfour to Sir Henry Clinton, received by the Amphitrite man of war, dated Charles-Town, April 7, 1781.

S I R,

I AM honoured with your letters of the 2d of January, and 19th of laft month ; as alfo with one of the 14th ult. by your Excellency's directions, from Captain Smith.

As Lord Cornwallis is in the greateft want of every fupply, I have fent him to Cape Fear what could be procured here, and as he will have many

calls

calls on the Hofpital, in confequence of the late marches and action, I have taken care to furnifh a fupply of officers and ftores to that department at Wilmington ; and fhall by that way forward to his Lordfhip *your Excellency's difpatches,* whenever an occafion offers.

PART VI.

PART VI.

CONTAINING

EXTRACTS

FROM THE

Correſpondence; between Lord Cornwallis's arrival at Wilmington, and his entering Virginia.

Extract. — *From Earl Cornwallis to Sir Henry Clinton, received by his Majeſty's ſhip Amphitrite, dated Camp, near Wilmington, April* 10, 1781.

SIR,

I AM juſt informed that I have a chance of sending a few lines to New-York by the Amphitrite But as it depends upon my being expeditious, I cannot attempt to give your Excellency a particular account of the winter's campaign, or the battle of Guildford.

I am

I am very anxious to receive your Excellency's commands, being as yet totally in the dark as to the intended operations of the fummer. I cannot help expreffing my wifhes that the Chefapeak may become the feat of war, even (if neceffary) at the expence of abandoning New-York. — Until Virginia is in a manner fubdued, our hold of the Carolinas muft be difficult, if not precarious. The rivers in Virginia are advantageous to an invading army; but North Carolina is, of all the provinces of America, the moft difficult to attack (unlefs material affiftance could be got from the inhabitants, the contrary of which I have fufficiently experienced) on account of its great extent, of the numberlefs rivers and creeks, and the total want of interior navigation.

Copy. — *Sir Henry Clinton to Earl Cornwallis, dated New-York, April 30, 1781.*

MY LORD,

CAPTAIN Biggs of his Majefty's fhip Amphi-trite, who arrived here the 22d, has delivered to me your Lordfhip's two letters from Wilmington of the 10th inftant, informing me of your having obtained a complete victory over the rebel General Greene, near Guildford, on the 15th ult. On which occa-

M fion

fion I beg leave to offer your Lordſhip my moſt hearty congratulations, and to requeſt you will preſent my thanks to Major-general Leſlie, Brigadier O'Hara, and Lieutenant-colonel Tarleton, for the great aſſiſtance you received from them, and to the officers and men under your command, for their great exertions on the march through Carolina, and their perſevering intrepidity in action.

The diſparity of numbers between your Lordſhip's force and that of the enemy oppoſed to you, appears to be very great; and I confeſs I am at ſome loſs to gueſs how your Lordſhip came to be reduced before the action to one thouſand three hundred and ſixty infantry, — as by the diſtribution ſent to me in your letter of the 6th of January, I am to ſuppoſe it was your intention to take with you the regiments mentioned in the margin ;* which (notwithſtanding the loſs of the ſeventy-firſt and legion, in the unfortunate affair of the Cowpens) I ſhould imagine muſt have amounted to conſiderably above three thouſand, excluſive of cavalry and militia.

Before I was favoured with your Lordſhip's letter, the rebel account of the battle of Guildford had led

me

* Brigade of guards.
Twenty-third.
Seventy-firſt, two battalions.
Jagers.
Regiment of Boſe.
Light infantry ſeventy-firſt.
Legion.
North Carolina regiment.

me indeed to hope that its confequences would have been more decifive; and that Green would have repaffed the Roanoke, and left your Lordfhip at liberty to purfue the objects of your move into North Carolina. Under the perfuafion therefore that you would foon be able to finifh your arrangements for the fecurity of the Carolinas, I fubmitted to you in my letter of the 13th inftant (a duplicate of which I have the honour to inclofe) the propriety in that cafe of your going in a frigate to Chefapeak, and directing fuch corps to follow you thither as you judged could be beft fpared. But as it is now probable that your Lordfhip's prefence in Carolina cannot be fo foon difpenfed with, I make no doubt but you will think it right to communicate to Major-general Phillips, without delay, the plan of your future operations in that quarter, together with your opinion how the Chefapeak army can beft direct theirs to affift them. That general officer has already under his orders three thoufand five hundred men, and I fhall fend him one thoufand feven hundred more, which are now embarked, and will fail whenever the Admiral is ready. With thefe, my Lord, which are rank and file fit for duty, and great part of them taken from the elite of my army, General Phillips is directed by his inftructions to act in favour of your Lordfhip to the beft of his own judgment, until he receives your orders; and afterwards in fuch manner as you

M 2   may

may pleafe to command him, &c. — But I fhall be forry to find your Lordfhip continue in the opinion that our hold of the Carolinas muft be difficult, if not precarious, until Virginia is in a manner fubdued; as that is an event which I fear would require a confiderable fpace of time to accomplifh; and as far as I can judge, it might be not quite fo expedient at this advanced feafon of the year to enter into a long operation in that climate. This, however will greatly depend upon circumftances, of which your Lordfhip and General Phillips may probably be better judges hereafter.

With regard to the operations of the fummer, which your Lordfhip is anxious to receive my directions about, you cannot but be fenfible that they muft in a great meafure depend on your Lordfhip's fucceffes in Carolina, the certainty and numbers of the expected reinforcement from Europe, and likewife your Lordfhip's fending back to me the corps I had fpared to you under Major-general Leflie (which Lord Rawdon in his letter of the 31ft of October told me you could return in the fpring) for until I am informed of the particulars of your Lordfhp's march through North Carolina, the effective ftrength of your moving army, your plan of operations for carrying thofe objects you had or may have in view into execution, as well by the corps acting under your immediate orders, as thofe acting in co-operation under Major-general Phillips, it muft be obvi-

 oufly

oufly impoffible for me to determine finally upon a plan of operations for the campaign.

I was indeed in great hopes that your fucceffes in North Carolina would have been fuch as to have put it in my power to avail myfelf of a large portion of your Lordfhip's army, the whole Chefapeak corps, and the reinforcements from Europe, for this campaign's operations to the northward of Carolina; but I obferve with concern from your Lordfhip's letter, that fo far from being in a condition to fpare me any part of your prefent force, you are of opinion that part of the European reinforcement will be indifpenfibly neceffary to enable you to act offenfively, or even to maintain yourfelf in the upper parts of the country.

Had I known what your Lordfhip's further offenfive meafures were intended to be for the remaining part of the feafon, I might now have given an opinion upon them, as well as on the probable co-operation of the corps in Chefapeak; without having which it will be fcarcely poffible for me to form any. For as I faid before, I fear no folid operation can be carried on to the northward of Chefapeak, before thofe to the fouthward of it are entirely at an end, either from fuccefs or the feafon; and my letter to your Lordfhip of the 6th of November will have informed you what were my ideas of the operations proper to be purfued in Chefapeak, and my expectations from them, had circumftances admitted of my

purfuing

purfuing the plan to its full extent. But I muft now defer the fixing ultimately on a plan for the campaign, until I am made acquainted with the final fuccefs of your Lordfhip's operations, your profpects and fentiments, and I can judge what force I can collect for fuch meafures as I can then determine upon.

I have the honour, &c.

(Signed)   H. CLINTON.

Copy. — From Lieutenant-colonel Balfour to Sir Henry Clinton, received by the Speedy packet, which called at Cape Fear, dated Charles-Town, April 20, 1781.

S I R,

I HAVE the honour to acquaint your Excellency, that by the letters from Lord Rawdon of the 12th, 13th, and 15th inftant, there is the fulleft information, that General Greene with his army is advancing into this province, and that his light troops have actually paffed the Pedee. The object of this movement there is every reafon to believe is Camden,

den, which at present is but weak, Lord Rawdon having detached Lieutenant-colonel Watson, with two battalions from that post ; so that in the end it may be expedient for combining our force, to relinquish every thing on the other side Santee — a measure, however, which your Excellency may be assured will not be taken but in case of the utmost necessity.

As this movement of Greene's may considerably change Lord Cornwallis's views, (who is now at Wilmington) I have judged it fit to lay before your Excellency as soon as possible this intelligence, which is like-wise forwarded to Lord Cornwallis by an express boat.

I have the honour, &c.

(Signed)   W. BALFOUR.

Extract of a letter from Lord Rawdon to Lord Corn-wallis, May 24, 1781.

Lieutenant-colonel Balfour was so good as to meet me at Nelson's. He took this measure that he might represent his circumstances to me. He stated that the revolt was universal, that from the little reason to apprehend this serious invasion,[*] *the old works of Charles-town had been in part levelled, to make*

* It is presumable that Colonel Balfour likewise communicated this material information to Lord Cornwallis,

*make way for new ones, which were not yet constructed;
that its garrison was inadequate to oppose any force of
consequence, and that the defection of the town's people
shewed itself in a thousand instances.* I agreed with
him in the conclusion to be drawn from thence, that
any misfortune happening to my corps might entail
the loss of the province.

———————————

*Copy.—Earl Cornwallis to Lord George Germain, dated
Wilmington, April* 23, 1781.

MY LORD,

I YESTERDAY received an express by a small
vessel from Charles-Town, informing me that a
frigate was there, but not then able to get over the
bar, with dispatches from Sir Henry Clinton, noti-
fying to me that Major-general Phillips had been detached into the Chesapeak with a considerable force,
with instructions to co-operate with this army, and
to put himself under my orders. This express likewise brought me the disagreeable accounts that the
upper posts of South Carolina were in the most imminent danger, from an alarming spirit of revolt
among many of the people, and by a movement of
General Greene's army.

                                                    Although

Although the expresses which I sent from Cross Creek, to inform Lord Rawdon of the necessity I was under of coming to this place, and to warn him of the possibility of such an attempt of the enemy, had all miscarried; yet his Lordship was lucky enough to be apprized of General Greene's approach, at least six days before he could possibly reach Camden; and I am therefore still induced to hope, from my opinion of his Lordship's abilities and the precautions taken by him and Lieutenant-colonel Balfour, that we shall not be so unfortunate as to lose any considerable corps.

The distance from hence to Camden, the want of forage and subsistence on the greatest part of the road, and the difficulty of passing the Pedee when opposed by an enemy, render it utterly impossible for me to give immediate assistance; and I apprehend a possibility of the utmost hazard to this little corps without the chance of a benefit in the attempt. For, if we are so unlucky as to suffer a severe blow in South Carolina, the spirit of revolt in that province would become very general, and the numerous rebels in this province be encouraged to be more than ever active and violent. This might enable General Greene to hem me in among the Great Rivers, and by cutting off our subsistence render our arms useless; and to remain here for transports to carry us off would be a work of time, would loose our cavalry, and be otherwise as ruinous and dis-

N   graceful

graceful to Britain as moft events could be. - I have therefore under fo many embarraffing circumftances (but *looking upon Charles-town as fafe from any immedi-ate attack of the rebels*) refolved to take advantage of General Greene's having left the back part of Virgi-nia open, and march immediately into that province, to attempt a junction with General Phillips.

I have more readily decided upon this meafure, be-caufe if General Greene fails in the object of his march, his retreat will relieve South Carolina; and my force being very infufficient for offenfive opera-tions in this province, may be employed ufefully in Virginia, in conjunction with the corps under the command of General Phillips.

I have the honour, &c.

(Signed)   CORNWALLIS.

———————

Copy. — From Earl Cornwallis to Sir Henry Clinton, dated Wilmington, April 24, 1781.

S I R,

I HAVE reflected very ferioufly on the fubject of my attempt to march into Virginia, and have in confequence written a letter to Major-general Phillips,

of

of which I have the honour to inclofe a copy to your Excellency.

I have likewife directed Lieutenant-colonel Balfour to fend tranfports and provifions to this port, in cafe I fhould find the junction with Major-general Phillips impracticable; and that I fhould have the mortification of feeing that there is no other method of conveying his Majefty's troops to South Carolina, without expofing them to the moft evident danger of being loft.

I have the honour, &c.

(Signed) CORNWALLIS,

Copy. — *From Earl Cornwallis to Major-general Phillips, dated April* 24, 1781.

DEAR PHILLIPS,

MY fituation here is very diftreffing, Greene took the advantage of my being obliged to come to this place, and has marched to South Carolina. My expreffes to Lord Rawdon on my leaving Crofs Creek, warning him of the poffibility of fuch a movement, have all failed ; mountaineers and militia have poured into the back part of that province, and I much fear that Lord Rawdon's pofts will be fo diftant from

N 2 each

each other, and his troops so scattered, as to put him in danger of being beat in detail ; and that the worst of consequences may happen to most of the troops out of Charles-town.

By a direct move towards Camden I cannot get time enough to relieve Lord Rawdon, and should he have fallen, my army would be exposed to the utmost danger, from the great rivers I should have to pass, the exhausted state of the country, the numerous militia, the almost universal spirit of revolt which prevails in South Carolina, and the strength of Greene's army, whose continentals alone are at least as numerous as I am : and I could be of no use on my arrival at Charles-town, there being nothing at present to apprehend for that post.　I shall therefore immediately march up the country by Duplin court house, pointing towards Hillsborough, in hopes to withdraw Greene.　If that should not succeed, I should be much tempted to try to make a junction with you. *The attempt is exceedingly hazardous, and many unforeseen difficulties may render it totally impracticable* ; so that you must not take any steps that may expose your army to the danger of being ruined.　I shall march to the lowest ford of the Roanoke, which I am informed is about twenty miles above Taylor's ferry. Send every possible intelligence to me by the cypher I inclose, and make every movement in your power to facilitate our meeting (which must be somewhere near Petersburg) with safety to your own army.　*I*
mention

mention the lowest ford, becaufe in a hoftile country, ferries cannot be depended upon ; but if I fhould decide upon the meafure of endeavouring to come to you, I fhall try to furprife the boats at fome of the ferries from Halifax, upwards, &c,

(Signed) CORNWALLIS.

Copy. — *From Lieutenant-colonel Balfour to Sir Henry Clinton, K. B. dated Charles-town, May 6,* 1781.

S I R,

IN my letters of the 20th and 23d ultimo, I had the honour to inform your Excellency, that our poft at Wright's bluff was invefted by the enemy, and the apprehenfions I was then under of Camden being in the fame fituation.

I am now to inform you that the former has fince been furrendered. The circumftances which led to this cannot be more fully explained, or with more honour to himfelf than by Lieutenant Mackay's journal of the fiege ; which together with the articles of capitulation, I therefore inclofe for your Excellency's infpection.

By to-morrow I am in hopes Lord Rawdon will be re-inforced by Lieutenant-colonel Watfon, with his corps and the fixty-fourth regiment.

4 But

But notwithstanding Lord Rawdon's brilliant success, I must inform your Excellency, that the general state of the country is most distressing; that the enemies parties are every where; the communication by land with Savannah no longer exists; Colonel Brown is invested at Augusta; and Colonel Cruger in the most critical situation at Ninety Six, nearly confined to his works, and without any present command over that country. Indeed I should betray the duty I owe your Excellency, did I not represent the defection of this province so universal, that I know of no mode short of depopulation, to retain it. This spirit of revolt is in a great measure kept up by the many officers prisoners of war here; and I should therefore think it advisable to remove them, as well as to make the most striking examples of such, as having taken protection, snatch every occasion to rise in arms against us.

I have the honour, &c.

(Signed) W. BALFOUR.

PART VII.

CONTAINING

EXTRACTS

FROM THE

Correspondence from his Lordſhip's entering Virginia, &c.

———————

Extract. — From Sir Henry Clinton, K. B. to Lord Cornwallis, dated New York, May 29, 1781.

MY LORD,   :

I HAD the honour of writing to your Lord-ſhip by Lord Chewton, who ſailed from hence in the Richmond the 4th inſtant to join you at Wilmington. But your Lordſhip's departure from thence will have prevented his meeting you there, and I hope he has ſince then joined you in the Cheſapeak.

When

When I firſt heard of your Lordſhip's retreat from Croſs Creek to Wilmington, I confeſs that I was in hopes you had reaſon to conſider Greene ſo totally hors de combat as to be perfectly at eaſe for Lord Rawdon's ſafety. And after your arrival at Wilmington, I flattered myſelf that if any change of circumſtances ſhould make it neceſſary, you could always have been able to march to the Walkamaw, where I imagined veſſels might have paſſed you over to George town. I cannot therefore conceal from your Lordſhip the apprehenſions I felt on reading your letter to me of the 24th ultimo ; wherein you informed me of the critical ſituation which you ſuppoſed the Carolinas to be in ; and that you ſhould probably attempt to effect a junction with Major general Phillips. Lord Rawdon's officer-like and ſpirited exertions, in taking advantage of Greene's having detached from his army, have indeed eaſed me of my apprehenſions for the preſent. But in the diſordered ſtate of Carolina and Georgia, as repreſented to me by Lieutenant-colonel Balfour, I ſhall dread what may be the conſequence of your Lordſhip's move ; unleſs a reinforcement arrives very ſoon in South Carolina, and ſuch inſtructions are ſent to the officer commanding there, as may induce him to exert himſelf in reſtoring tranquility to that province at leaſt. Theſe, I make no doubt your Lordſhip has already ſent to Lord Rawdon, and that every neceſſary meaſure for this purpoſe

poſe will be taken by his Lordſhip in conſequence of them, ſhould he remain in the command. ——————

—————— Had it been poſſible for your Lordſhip, in your letter of the 10th ultimo, to have intimated the probability of your intention to form a junction with General Phillips, I certainly ſhould have endeavoured to have ſtopped you —————— as I did then, as well as now, conſider ſuch a move as like to be dangerous to our intereſts in the ſouthern colonies. And this, my Lord, was not my only fear. For I will be free' to own that I was apprehenſive for the corps under your Lordſhip's immediate orders, as well as for that under Lord Rawdon. And I ſhould not have thought even the one under Major-general Phillips in ſafety at Peterſburg, at leaſt for ſo long a time, had I not fortunately on hearing of your being at Wilmington, ſent another detachment from this army, to reinforce him.

I am perſuaded your Lordſhip will have the goodneſs to excuſe my ſaying thus much. But what is done cannot now be altered. And as your Lord-ſhip has thought proper to make this deciſion, I ſhall moſt gladly avail myſelf of your very able aſſiſtance, in carrying on ſuch operations *as you ſhall judge beſt in Virginia,* until we are compelled, as I fear we muſt be, by the climate, to bring them more northward. Your Lordſhip will have been informed of my ideas reſpecting operations to the northward of the Caroli-nas, by my inſtructions to the different General offi-

O   cers

cers detached to the Chefapeak, and the fubftance of fome converfations with General Phillips on the fubject, which I committed to writing, and fent to him with my laft difpatch, with directions to communicate it to your Lordfhip. By thefe your Lordfhip will obferve that my firft object has been to co-operate with your meafures. But your Lordfhip's fituation at different periods made it neceffary for me occafionally to vary my inftructions to thofe General officers, according to circumftances. They were originally directed to affift your Lordfhip's operations in fecuring South and recovering North Carolina; their attention was afterwards pointed to the faving South Carolina.

And now, your Lordfhip may think it neceffary to employ your force in recovering both or either of thefe provinces, by either a direct or indirect operation. With refpect to the firft your Lordfhip muft be fole judge. With refpect to the laft you have my opinions. *My opinions may however probably give way to yours fhould they differ from them, as they will have the advantage of being formed on the fpot, and upon circumftances which at this diftance I cannot of courfe judge of. I fhall therefore leave them totally to your Lordfhip to decide upon, till you either hear from me or we meet.*

I fhould be happy to be able to afcertain the time when our reinforcements may arrive; but as I have received no letters from the minifter of a later date

2   than

than the 7th of February, I am at a lofs to guefs how foon we may expect them. As I had judged the force I fent to the Chefapeak fully fufficient for all operations there, even though we fhould extend them to the experiment (mentioned in the converfations referred to) at the weftern head of the Chefapeak, a-bout Baltimore, &c. And your Lordfhip will per-ceive that it was General Phillips and Arnold's opi-nion they were fufficient for even that on the eaftern, (which however might certainly require a greater force), it is poffible that the additional corps your Lordfhip has brought with you may enable you to return fomething to me for this poft. But I beg your Lordfhip will by no means confider this as a call — for I fhould rather content myfelf with ever fo bare a defenfive, until there was an appearance of ferious operation againft me, than cramp your's in the leaft. But (as I faid in a former letter) I truft to your Lordfhip's difintereftednefs, that you will not require from me more troops than what are abfolutely want-ed ; and that you will recollect a circumftance, which I am ever aware of, in carrying on operations in the Chefapeak ; *which is that they can be no longer fecure than while we are fuperior at fea.* That we fhall re-main fo I moft fincerely *hope* — nor have I any reafon to fufpect we fhall not ; but at all events I may at leaft expect timely information will be fent me of the contrary being likely to happen. In which cafe I hope your Lordfhip may be able *to place your army in*

O 2 *a fecure*

a secure situation during such temporary inconvenience. For should it become permanent, I need not say what our prospects in this country are likely to be. The admiral being now off the Hook gives me an opportunity of communicating with him by letter, and I have in the most pressing terms requested his attention to the Chesapeak; having repeatedly told him, that should the *enemy possess it even for forty-eight hours, your Lordship's operations there may be exposed to most imminent danger.* General Robertson has also endeavoured to impress him with the same ideas. But until I have an answer in writing, I cannot be sure that he will, as I do, consider the Chesapeak as the first object: For he at present seems rather inclined to lead his fleet to open the port of Rhode-island, and to cruise to the northward of Nantucket for a fleet, which he has heard is coming from Europe with a small reinforcement to the French armament, and which I am of opinion is bound to Rhode-island. I have however taken every occasion to represent to him the necessity of hearty co-operation and communication. If they fail, I am determined it shall not be on my side.

I have the honour, &c.

(Signed)   H. CLINTON.

[Sent by Lieutenant-colonel M'Pherson, in the Loyalist, June 15.]

Extract.

Extract. — *From Earl Cornwallis to Sir Henry Clinton, K. B. dated Bird's Plantation, North of James-river, May 26, 1781.*

SIR,

THE arrival of the reinforcement has made me easy about Portsmouth for the present. I have sent General Leslie thither with the seventeenth regiment, and the two battalions of Anspach, keeping the forty-third regiment with the army.

I shall now proceed to dislodge La Fayette from Richmond, and with my light troops to destroy any magazines or stores in the neighbourhood, which may have been collected either for his use, or for General Greene's army. From thence I purpose to move to the neck at Williamsburgh, which is represented as healthy, and where some subsistence may be procured; and keep myself unengaged from operations, which might interfere with your plan for the campaign, until I have the satisfaction of hearing from you. I hope I shall then have an opportunity to receive better information than has hitherto been in my power to procure, relative to a proper harbour and place of arms. At present I am inclined to think well of York. The objections to Portsmouth are, that it cannot be made strong without an army to defend it; that it is remarkably unhealthy; and can

give

give no protection to a ship of the line. Wayne has not yet joined La Fayette, nor can I positively learn where he is, or what is his force. Greene's cavalry are said to be coming this way; but I have no certain accounts of it.

Your Excellency desires Generals Phillips and Arnold to give you their opinions relative to Mr. ———'s proposal. As General Arnold goes to New-York by the first safe conveyance, you will have an opportunity of hearing his sentiments in person. Experience has made me less sanguine, and more arrangements seem to me necessary for so important an expedition than appears to occur to General Arnold.

Mr. ———'s conversations bear too great a resemblance to those of the emissaries from North Carolina, to give me much confidence; and from the experience I have had, and the dangers I have undergone, one maxim appears to me to be absolutely necessary for the safe and honourable conduct of this war; which is, that we should have as few posts as possible; and that wherever the King's troops are, they should be in respectable force. By the vigorous exertions of the present governors of America, large bodies of men are soon collectd, and I have too often observed, that when a storm threatens, our friends disappear.

In regard to taking possession of Philadelphia by an incursion (even if practicable) without an intention

of

of keeping or burning it, (neither of which appear to be adviſeable) I ſhould apprehend it would do more harm than good to the cauſe of Britain.

I ſhall take the liberty of repeating, that if offenſive war is intended, Virginia appears to me to be the only province in which it can be carried on; and in which there is a ſtake. But to reduce the province and keep poſſeſſion of the country, a conſiderable army would be neceſſary; for with a ſmall force, the buſineſs would probably terminate unfavourably, though the beginning might be ſucceſsful. In caſe it is thought expedient, and a proper army for the attempt can be formed; I hope your Excellency will do me the juſtice to believe, that I neither wiſh nor expect to have the command of it, leaving you at New York on the defenſive. Such ſentiments are ſo far from my heart, that I can with great truth aſſure you, that few things could give me greater pleaſure, than being relieved by your preſence, from a ſituation of ſo much anxiety and reſponſibility.

By my letter of the 20th, your Excellency will obſerve, that inſtead of thinking it poſſible to do any thing in North Carolina, I am of opinion that it is doubtful whether we can keep the poſts in the back parts of South Carolina. And I believe I have ſtated in former letters, the infinite difficulty of protecting a frontier of three hundred miles, againſt a perſevering enemy, in a country where we have no water communication,

munication, and where few of the inhabitants are active or useful friends.

In enumerating the corps employed in the southern district, your Excellency will recollect that they are all very weak ; and that some of the British as well as Provincial regiments, retain nothing but the name. Our weakness at Guildford was not owing to any detachment, unless that with the baggage, but to losses by action, sickness, &c. during the winter's campaign.

Extract. — *Sir Henry Clinton, K. B. to Lord Cornwallis, dated New-York, June* 11, 1781.

RESPECTING my opinions of stations in James and York rivers, I shall beg leave only to refer your Lordship to my instructions to, and correspondence with, Generals Phillips and Arnold, together with the substance of my conversations with the former ; which your Lordship will have found amongst General Phillips's papers, and to which I referred you in my last dispatch ; I shall therefore of course approve of any alterations your Lordship may think proper to make in those stations.

The

The detachments I have made from this army into Cheſapeak ſince General Leſlie's expedition in October laſt, incluſive, have amounted to ſeven thouſand ſeven hundred and twenty-four effectives ; and at the time your Lordſhip made the junction with the corps there, there were under Major-general Phillips's orders, five thouſand three hundred and four. A force, I ſhould have hoped would be ſufficient of itſelf to carry on any operations in any of the ſouthern provinces in America.

———— comparing, therefore the force under your Lordſhip, and that of the enemy oppoſed to you (and I think it clearly appears they have, for the preſent, no intention of ſending thither reinforcement) I ſhould have hoped you would have quite ſufficient to carry on any operation in Virginia — ſhould that have been adviſable in this advanced ſeaſon.

By the intercepted letters incloſed to your Lordſhip in my laſt diſpatch, you will obſerve, that I am threatened with a ſiege in this poſt. My preſent effective force is only ten thouſand nine hundred and thirty-one. With reſpect to what the enemy may collect for ſuch an object, it is probable they may amount to at leaſt twenty thouſand ; beſides reinforcement to the French (which from pretty good authority, I have reaſon to expect) and the numerous militia of the five neighbouring provinces.

Thus

Thus circumftanced, I am perfuaded your Lordfhip will be of opinion, that the fooner I concentrate my force the better. Therefore, (unlefs your Lordfhip, after the receipt of my letters of the 29th of May and 8th inft. fhould incline to agree with me in opinion, and judge it rightto adopt my ideas refpecting the move to Baltimore, or the Delaware Neck, &c.) I beg léave to recommend it to you, as foon as you have finifhed the active operations you may be now engaged in, to take a defenfive ftation in any healthy fituation you choofe (be it at Williamfburgh or York town) and I would wifh in that cafe, that after referving to yourfelf fuch troops as you may judge neceffary for an ample defenfive, and defultory move. ments by water, for the purpofe of annoying the enemy's communications, deftroying magazines, &c. the following corps may be fent to me in fucceffion, as you can fpare them :

    Two battalions of light infantry.

    Forty-third regiment.

    Seventy-fixth, or eightieth.

    Two battalions of Anfpach.

    Queen's rangers, cavalry and infantry.

    Remains of the detachment of the feventeenth light dragoons.

And fuch a proportion of artillery as can be fpared, particularly men.

Copy. — Sir Henry Clinton, K. B. to Lord Cornwallis, dated New-York, June 15, 1781.

MY LORD,

As the Admiral has thought proper to ſtop the ſailing of the convoy with ſtores, horſe, accoutrements, &c. (which has been for ſome days ready to ſail to the Cheſapeak) without aſſigning to me any reaſon for, ſo doing, I delay not a moment to diſpatch a runner to your Lordſhip with a duplicate of my letter of the 11th inſt. which was to go by that opportunity. And as I am led to ſuppoſe from your Lordſhip's letter of the 26th ultimo, that you may not think it expedient to adopt the operations I had recommended in the Cheſapeak, and will by this time probably have finiſhed thoſe you were engaged in; I requeſt you will immediately embark a part of the troops, ſtated in the letter incloſed; beginning with the light infantry; and ſend them to me with all poſſible diſpatch; for which purpoſe Captain Hudſon, or officer commanding the king's ſhips, will, I preſume, upon your Lordſhip's application appoint a proper convoy. I ſhall likewiſe, in proper time, ſolicit the admiral to ſend ſome more tranſports to the Cheſapeak; in which your Lordſhip will pleaſe to ſend hither the remaining troops you judge can be ſpared from the defence of the poſts you may occupy, as I do not think it adviſeable to leave more

troops

troops in that unhealthy climate, at this feafon of the year, than what are abfolutely wanted for a defenfive, and defultory water excurfions.

H. CLINTON,

Extract. — *Lord Cornwallis to Sir Henry Clinton, K. B. dated Williamfbugrh, June* 30, 1781.

————BEING in the place of General Phillips, I thought myfelf called upon by you, to give my opinion, with all deference, on Mr. ———'s propofals, and the attempt upon Philadelphia. Having experienced much difappointment on that head, I own I would cautioufly engage in meafures, depending materially for their fuccefs, upon active affiftance from the country. And I thought the attempt on Philadelphia would do more harm than good to the caufe of Great Britain.

———— However, my opinion on that fubject is at prefent of no great importance, as it appears from your Excellency's difpatches, that in the execution of thofe ideas, a co-operation was intended from your fide; which now could not be depended upon from the

un-

uncertainty of the permancy of our naval ſuperiority, and your apprehenſions of an intended ſerious attempt upon New York.

END OF THE APPENDIX.

Return of intrenching Tools in the possession of the Engineers at York Town, in Virginia on the 23d of August, 1781.

Spades and shovels	-	-	-		400
Pick-axes	-	-	-	-	190
Felling-axes	-	-	-	-	210
Hand-hatchets	-	-	-		160
Wheel-barrows	-	-	-		32
					992

New-York,   OL. DE LANCY,

Dec. 27, 1781.   ADJUTANT-GENERAL.

N. B. This return formed from different returns, signed by Lieutenant Sutherland, Lord Cornwallis's principal Engineer in the Chesapeak.

VIEW

www.ingramcontent.com/pod-product-compliance
Lightning Source LLC
Chambersburg PA
CBHW020234030726
47497CB00009B/3097